WAITING on WOMEN

GP Lane

For Frank and Agnes Lane; without whom,
I would not be possible.

Aside from Synchronicity/Serendipity, the four other stories are pure
works of fiction. Any similarity to real persons, living or dead, is
coincidental and not intended by the author.

ISBN: 0615988482
ISBN 13: 9780615988481
Library of Congress Control Number: 2014904675
LCCN Imprint Name: GP Lane, Peconic, New York

TABLE OF CONTENTS

SERENDIPITY/SYNCHRONICITY

(The White Rabbit sings)
I'm late
I'm late
For a very important date
No time to say "Hello," "Goodbye,"
I'm late, I'm late, I'm late!
                —Sammy Fain and Bob Hilliard, Disney's *Alice in Wonderland*

She was not in the lobby. She was not at the bar. And for a split second, I thought that I was not at the Ritz.

It was a simple plan. A late May date with my sister. We were to meet at the Columbus Circle entrance to Central Park and stroll through the park dressed in summer attire. Lunch was to be somewhere on the West Side. Afterward, we would saunter across the park to the museum, explore one specific gallery, and then have cocktails at the Stanhope followed by a quick walk downtown to the Ritz for lobster rolls before an early evening concert at Carnegie Hall. I signed on as soon as she suggested it and eagerly awaited the date. I do not see my sister often enough and this was to be a gift for us both.

"What will you wear?" she asked.

"Why do we need to costume ourselves?"

"It's the beginning of summer…it'll be fun. Don't be such a dick!"

The phone conversations prior to the event frequently ended this way.

1

"How about I buy one of those tuxedo T-shirts and wear it with my old pair of ripped denims?"

"Didn't you hear me say not to be such a dick?" Her voice drifted; she said something to her kids and came back with, "Why don't you buy yourself a seersucker suit?"

I had toyed with the idea for quite some time. I always liked seersucker suits, and, after all, it is a quintessential summer look. I bought a brown one and added a linen shirt, silk suspenders, matching bow tie, nylon socks in the palest beige, and brown wing-tip shoes. All I needed was a boater and hooked cane, and I could have been cast as Harold Hill in a local production of *The Music Man*. But without those last two items, I did look quite dashing. If my sister was accurate in her description of the breezy summer dress she'd bought in Paris, we ought to turn heads on our date, looking like a couple from times gone by, out for an afternoon stroll through the park.

I kept the suit as a surprise. I told her to wear her frock and from her description of it suggested she invest in a parasol in case the sun was too hot and she was overcome by the vapors. When she became too obnoxious, I'd threaten her with the tuxedo T-shirt, and my jeans became more ripped depending upon her level of irritability. It's just the relationship we have.

The concert was to be a performance, by an orchestra and a gigantic chorus, of the musical scores of two films, *The Lion in Winter* and the silent classic *Ivan the Terrible*. *The Lion in Winter* was our favorite film. It starred Katharine Hepburn, Peter O'Toole, and a young Anthony Hopkins. It tells the story of England's King Henry II, his imprisoned wife Eleanor, and their three sons: Richard (the Lionhearted), Geoffrey (Duke of Brittany), and John (the nasty king from the Robin Hood story, famous for signing the Magna Carta). It is full of acerbic lines and amusing dysfunctional family situations, something we both could relate to. The film is set one particular Christmas ('tis why Eleanor is out of prison), when the aging King of England has a ceremonial meeting with the new King of France, Philip (played wonderfully by Timothy Dalton), to discuss boundaries, broken promises, and which son will succeed to the aging king's throne. They all bicker, and play one another, as we, the audience, get an inside view of such regal business. I must repeat: that film has a lot of great lines, and my sister and I know most of them.

The day arrived with a clear sky and a forecast of delicious perfection: low seventies, sunshine all day, and a cool coastal breeze—a comfortable day that made it easy to dress in my costume. I straightened my tie (it had taken nine attempts to get it tied correctly) in the reflective glass outside the station. Although my hair could have used cutting, I thought it gave me a relaxed air.

I hate the cell phone. No, I hate all phones, but the cell, in particular, is just a nuisance, and in this outfit it was anachronistic as well. My sister and I were to meet at 1:00 p.m., and as my train pulled into Penn Station, the blasted thing announced I had three messages.

Something magical happens when you leave the artificial light of an underground station and emerge into the brilliant sunlight and onto the streets of New York City. I remember I took in the sights and scents of that day and oddly thought, *home.* I was born here but left as a child. I know that had I been allowed in that decision process, my vote would have been cast to stay in this exciting city.

Two messages were unlistenable, disjointed sounds as if someone were slowly choking on a bit of beef or being choked by a thick-mitted psychopath. The third was from a good friend who was watching my terrier who told me that if I ever wanted to ditch the little devil, they'd take him in a heartbeat. It was sweet, but at the end of it there was this: "Your sister called, but I couldn't make out a word she said. Maybe you should call her?" And I did, but only her voicemail answered. I left a message saying, "I'm here...I can't wait to see you."

It has been my custom to grab a slice of pizza at a little place that bustles with constant business at Ninth and Thirty-Eighth. I decided against that, knowing I'd be lunching at a brasserie I liked and not wanting to spoil my appetite. Besides, I couldn't risk a stain on the suit. People noticed me in this costume, and two actually remarked, "Nice suit," as they passed me. I nodded and smiled.

Waiting for my sister was nothing new. She had a reputation for perpetual lateness. One hour passed and my anxiety had me leave a rather terse message. "Sweetness, I'm here waiting. If I knew you were going to be this late, I would have brought a boater to protect my naked head from the sun and a cane to bloody that pretty dress of yours!" Hunger got the better of me, and after an additional forty-five minutes, I proceeded to the restaurant alone. I knew she'd breeze in with some excuse, and we'd still have a pleasant day.

Beer has always been delicious to me, and as I decided what to eat, I drank one with the thirst of a man ready for more than one. Perhaps it was my disposition; perhaps it was the Irish in me. I ordered lunch, and, while I waited, had a second icy one. The alcohol dulled my fevered brain.

Lunch was superb: hanger steak (rare), frites, and a splendid salad of field greens, sweetened pecans, and pears with blue cheese crumbled on top. I paid the bill and felt little or no pain as I began to cross the park. Shirtless men played flag football on the great lawn, teenagers flew by on skateboards, and there was even a young man who struggled with a box kite. I took it all in and wondered what the *hell* had happened to my sister. Each message from her sounded like it was transmitted from a basement cell in a gulag. A steady hiss crackled while snippets of her voice snapped in and out; all were gibberish. Whatever had detained her must have been huge, as it was the longest I'd ever waited for her. Had it been anyone else, I'd have been long gone.

But, I really didn't wait after all: I went through the park, drank copious amounts of water, visited the museum, and saw an exhibit by a gentleman I had known for years. It was a thrill to see his work on the walls of the Met. I had turned off my phone as not to be an obnoxious lout who interrupted the peace with a one-sided conversation, but I turned the phone back on as I flew down the steps of the Met, crossed Fifth Avenue, and walked over to the comforting sanctuary of the bar of the Stanhope. There were five messages. I checked the call list and saw that three were from my sister, one was from a good friend who knew I was in town, and the last was from a number unfamiliar to me. The first three needed to be erased: complete garbled noise. The fourth was from my friend Trish saying I should hop in a cab and meet her at the Jane Street Tavern for a drink. The last one, the one I was curious about, was actually from my sister. She said she used a stranger's phone and had tried to reach me all day to give me the list of reasons (all legitimate, all ignored by me) as to why she was late. It ended with, "I'll be at the Ritz by five, and I promise I'll make it up to you." I wanted to call the stranger and ask him or her to relay a message: You can't make up lost time.

That is just how time works. Seconds pass, and then minutes, and before you know it, hours are gone with no hope ever getting all that time back.

I remember my reaction as if it were happening now. I looked at my watch: 4:20 p.m. I looked up to the blue, blue sky and took a deep breath. I hoped that my reddened face wouldn't frighten the Stanhope's barman, Harold. I went in and ordered a dirty martini. Harold and I shook hands as I exchanged pleasantries with the finest mixologist in all of Manhattan. I breathed the room in and thought: *Fuck her. She can wait for me now!*

The martini was perfection in an icy glass. Harold left me a bowl of smoked almonds, though I'd have preferred some cold shrimp and thought about ordering some. I forgot to turn off the phone, and as it began to ring its stupid ringtone, I flipped it and saw that the caller was my sister. I turned the detestable thing to vibrate. I ordered a second martini and by 5:00 p.m. was pleasantly and most definitely drunk. Not sloppy, fall-down drunk, but drunk enough to let my anger brew.

The quickest route would be to go downtown to Fifty-Ninth, cross it by the Plaza Hotel, and onto Central Park South. The Ritz-Carlton was close. I opted to cut through the park, and although I had quit smoking cigarettes some time before, I asked a well-dressed lady smoking a Gauloises if I could steal one. "You obviously do not know what it means to steal, Monsieur. You may have one of my cigarettes."

The first filter-less puff was bliss. As the familiar blue smoke left my lungs, I thanked the lady, crossed Fifth, and headed into the park. Normally I'd take in the sights and sounds, but as I made my way along twisted paths, I consumed myself with witty one-liners regarding my sister's lateness. They ranged from her insulting my summer suit to my stammering interruptions while she presented her reasons for being more than four hours late—the latest she's ever been for anyone.

I had sobered enough from the walk and fury that when I arrived at the door of the Ritz, I was calm and eager to pounce on her with my verbal assault. First, I stopped at the restroom and washed my hands. They reeked of cigarettes. It was cool and comfortable there, and the gentleman who handed me a towel remarked that when he was a boy, a seersucker suit was a perfect look for summer, "Still is. It's nice that you youngsters are bringing it back." (Youngster? Mind you, I was in my forties!)

I received a finally discernible phone message: "Lovey? I'm so, so sorry! The train is stuck outside of Penn, and I don't know when I'll be in town. I'll be there soon. Promise. Have a cold one waiting for me."

A cold what? Beer? Martini? Shoulder? I ordered a dirty martini and did what I had done all day: waited. What else was I to do? I wanted to storm out and eat another steak. The martini was perfectly dirty. I asked for a glass of water and stared off into the busy lobby full of well-dressed people—not one in a seersucker suit.

In a moment I saw her there, looking up at the lobby clock and then into the bar. She was a vision of spring. Her dress was a sheer white layered thing with small bunches of violets puckered all over it. There was the smallest ruffle that framed her neck and disappeared into her décolletage. Oddly, a parasol would have worked, but instead she held a purse that was round and soft, like a cinched sack stuffed with marbles. The inference of a ruffle hemmed the dress's full skirt and in that light, her skin, hair, and bright smile melted my alcoholic rage. Both men and women who passed looked upon her with obvious delight. She peered over their expressions and searched for me. I was tempted to hide, but instead, stood and greeted her. We embraced. I whispered softly in her ear.

"How dear of you to let me out of prison; like school you keep me young." It was a line from *The Lion in Winter*.

"I'm so sorry."

"Enough. You're here now. Great dress."

"This old thing?" She couldn't help herself and continued Gloria Grahame's line from *It's a Wonderful Life*. "Why, I only wear it when I don't care how I look!"

We sat and I ordered her a glass of champagne. Silently we sipped our drinks, and she realized how drunk I was from my glazed expression and reddened cheeks.

"Not another word." I said nothing. She pulled at my lapel and said, "Come. We'll eat something in the lobby. Leave your drink. You've had enough."

She was right, of course. I had had enough, but it wasn't the alcohol. I took her fisted hand off my suit and left enough cash on the bar to more than cover the bill. Petulantly, I lifted my drink, swallowed the contents, but did not eat the olive. *Ha! That'll show her!*

The lobby was elegantly comfortable. I actually considered taking off my shoes and loosening my tie to lie upon the soft upholstered loveseat. "If you even unlace one shoe, I'll smack you with my purse." It was small and dense: I couldn't risk a black eye. She ordered way too much food: lobster roll, turkey club, and for starters, cold shrimp, spring rolls, and a smoked salmon platter. I was to drink no more alcohol. "You've had enough!" This did not stop me. After the waiter brought the first course, I ignored my sister and ordered a Stella.

At one point during the litany as to why she was late, all my one-liners blew away like the blue smoke of that French cigarette (of which I wished I had another). "Cancer...friend...needed a ride...doctor...line work at my usual train depot...." She went on and on, and I let her. Then, as I sipped my beer, she asked what I had done all those hours alone.

Before I could retrieve any of my wit, a well-dressed man of about sixty leaned over my sister, kissed her upon her head, and began speaking French. It was an acquaintance of hers, Henri. I excused myself and went to the little shop inside the hotel and, of course, bought a pack of those filter-less cigarettes. The first one was not as pleasant as the earlier one, but it did quell something ugly inside of me.

When I returned Henri was gone, and she rummaged through her purse. Her desperate eyes looked up, and I knew she'd lost or forgotten the tickets.

This is where I began to lose my calm. "What? Look again."

I would have probably exploded if the server hadn't arrived with the rest of our food. Beside the two sandwiches there was a platter of three mini-burgers that hadn't been ordered. They had been a mistake, and the chef had sent them out to the man in the seersucker suit. I love the Ritz! Luck shone her beneficent smile upon us, and there, inside a zippered pocket, were the tickets.

"Good," I said. "Now I don't have to kill you."

Between the three plates were so many frites that I felt the alcohol lose its precious grip under a heavy dose of carbohydrates. I longed to lie upon the couch, unlace these wingtips, and unleash my "dogs." All that strolling had taken its toll. Instead I ate with the enthusiasm of a ravenous teenage boy. She sipped her wine and nibbled on a fry or two. When I remarked that she should eat something, she babbled something in French that I completely missed. The lobster was buttery and plump. The turkey club was heaven (real turkey breast slices, not that deli meat product) with hickory-smoked bacon crunchier than the lettuce. And the burgers—well, let me state here and now; that the two I consumed were everything White Castle burgers are supposed to be. The roll, onions, melted cheese, and burger itself were each a revelation. I would have eaten the third if not for my sister, who hunched over the low table to not get any burger juice on her blousy frock. I, on the other hand, avoided any stains by using excessive amounts of cloth napkins draped across my suit. It made me look like a really odd quilt. I was not allowed to pay for this meal. I put up no protest. The check had to have been substantial; after all, we were at the Ritz.

The early evening cool of the city wafted over me, reminding me I was drunk. The food sobered me a bit but not enough to be the proverbial judge. We were not late, but not early either; it would take fifteen or so minutes to get to Carnegie Hall. It was a short distance, so walking one way or another made little difference.

At the corner of Sixth and Fifty-Seventh, she grabbed my jacket and pulled at me to cross the street, saying, "Come, my little brother." (I'm older.) "Now see here, boy!" she added, quoting from *The Lion in Winter.*

I swept my arm and disconnected her grabby clutch. With every bit of righteous indignation I had in me, I snarled, "I am a king! I am no man's 'boy'!"

She doesn't miss a beat with the reply Peter O'Toole spat out in the movie: "A king? Because you put your ass on purple cushions?"

There are encapsulated moments: Times when something monumental happens. Sound diminishes. Sights blur. While you and possibly another are in a cocoon where only you exist. This was one of those moments; something precious; a gift of an experience that lives on in memory until death… and maybe thereafter. Who really knows?

A man, older than my sister and I, attired in a tan trench coat, turned, looked at us both, and said, "I directed that scene."

If my expression was anything akin to my sister's, it was this: wide-eyed stare, jaws dropped as we glanced at each other and then at the gentleman, back to each other, and…again at the gentleman. And then, being so taken off guard by this man's pronouncement, I, with an arsenal of language at my disposal, the wit of Oscar Wilde, Noel Coward, Edward Albee, Dorothy Parker, and the great Shakespeare himself, I (and I am embarrassed to admit this) with the back of my right hand, slapped the gentleman on his shoulder, and said, "Get da fuck *outta* here!" I never speak like that. It is so Brooklyn. So New *Yawk*!

My sister came to my side as the gentleman extended his hand with, "Really, I'm Anthony Harvey, and I directed Peter O'Toole and Timothy Dalton in that movie."

My sister, stunned by this chance encounter, was silent as I once again slapped at the man's shoulder and repeated, "Get da *fuck* outta here!"

"I'm actually on my way to hear a concert." My sister grabbed my arm before I had the chance to assault Mr. Harvey a third time.

"How lovely to meet you, Mr. Harvey…. My brother and I are going to that very same concert."

"You know," said Mr. Anthony Harvey, director of our favorite film, "I've heard people quote that movie often, but never that quote."

The light changed and before he left for Carnegie Hall, we shook his hand and thanked him for directing what we consider one of the best films of the twentieth century.

He smiled, looked me up and down, and remarked, "Great suit." Then Mr. Anthony Harvey disappeared into and among the pedestrians as we, my sister and I, stared each other down in disbelief.

"Serendipity," she announced.

I looked at her and replied, "No, synchronicity."

If she hadn't been so very late, if I hadn't been so very drunk and surly, we probably would never have met Anthony Harvey…. We would never have had that experience. All the elements of space and time, of circumstance and yes, serendipity, fell so neatly into place that for the rest of the evening we were giddy with awe. We cherished the music that night, the orchestra was superb, and the chorus filled the house with a glorious sound that resounded through my very being. It resounds with me still. The film clips sparked their familiarity, and the experience was bliss. Looking back, as I often do, I remember every bit of that day. But mostly I remember my sister—perpetually late, yet always well worth the wait.

TABLE 64

But maybe I ought to practice a little now?
So people who know me are not too shocked and surprised
When suddenly I am old, and start to wear purple.

—Jenny Joseph, "Warning"

Marco's is an Italian-American restaurant that seats 180 diners. It is rarely seated to capacity but is always busy. Located between Park and Madison avenues, it hums with steady business from 1:00 p.m. until midnight, when the kitchen officially closes. Not often, but once in a while, Marco himself will cook an entire meal with the assistance of Emilio, his sous chef. Usually this is for a select clientele, and the profit margin is substantial. There is a courtyard for such occasions, so Marco will take the reins only in late spring, summer, or early fall, depending upon the weather and his mood.

The success of Marco's lies in the ease with which his restaurant runs. He'll sometimes remark, "My restaurant is a well-oiled machine.... And the oil is of course—olive!" He usually laughs a bit too loud at his own joke, but his laugh is nonetheless sincere and is often infectious.

Marco Pollintini stands five foot seven in his stocking feet, but he is five nine and a half with the lifts his brother Stefano glues into his hand-crafted shoes. Stefano, if you haven't guessed, is an old-world-style shoemaker with a small factory and shop in Milan. He specializes in only men's footwear, and his product is a step above (no pun intended) other shoes you may find while strolling the cobbled streets of Marco's hometown. Once a year Stefano will come to New York, stay with his brother and mother for a few days, and then fly out west. Stefano is fascinated by the American Southwest. Arizona, New Mexico, and Texas are the three states he travels to most, and he usually makes many friends along the way. Stefano spends long hours working, so when he is on his yearly jaunt out west he lets loose, and these are his words, "in a big, American way." Stefano always laughs a big hearty laugh when he says this. His laugh is deep and infectious, and like his brother Marco, it is sincere.

It is Stefano who encourages Marco to add big, juicy sirloin burgers to both his lunch and dinner menus. It is Stefano, as well, who suggests Constance Cunningham and her lady friends drop on by Marco's, if they're ever in New York City. Stefano assures her, in no uncertain terms, that she will be welcome, "like a long, steady summer rain during drought season, ma'am!" His Texas drawl intermingled with his thick Italian accent makes for an interesting sound. It is indescribable. You really need to hear it to believe it.

And today Stefano's invitation will be acted upon, and Marco's generous and easygoing way will be tested. Without reservations or even the benefit of a phone call, Constance Cunningham, whose family owns a cattle ranch just outside of Angelina County, and who, unbeknownst to Marco, had the most satisfying sexual experience of her fifty-three-year life with Stefano just a few months ago, bursts through the etched glass entry doors of Marco's Italian-American Restaurant.

She is a tall woman. In flats, she is five foot ten, but in her bright red, hand-tooled cowboy boots, she is an easy six feet and towers over Marco Pollintini. He does not know what to make of this large, imposing woman. She is dressed all in purple, deep purple, and although her outfit must be expensive from all the white embroidery and fringe, to Marco, who is used to a more conservatively dressed clientele, it is about the most tasteless dress he has ever seen. Atop her head is a bright red Stetson festooned with purple and white feathers in the band. Still, she is a handsome woman. She has strong features and big, deep brown eyes that brighten whenever she smiles. She nods at the hostess, Amy, who stares in disbelief at the sight of Ms. Constance Cunningham from the great state of Texas.

"Marco Pollintini?" Her accent is thick and she elongates that last syllable so Amy hears: Marco Pollin-teeenie!

12

Marco, who sees her entrance from behind the bar, and hears her stretching out his name like she's mocking it (which she is not), waits for Amy to call him. He hears Amy's sweet, youthful voice direct this imposing figure into the bar, where Enzo, the barman, is restocking shelves and Marco is reviewing the day's reservations.

"Mr. Poll-in-teeeenni?" She is looking directly at Enzo; then, realizing her mistake, she turns toward Marco, who is already standing and walking toward her.

"Signora, how may I help you?"

They shake hands and he looks up and into those dark eyes, nearly forgetting the garish purple frock she wears. He pulls back and takes her into his smile. As she begins to identify herself, he leads her to a cozy, dimly lit bar table with a single white rosebud floating in a glass bowl.

She starts speaking immediately. "Oh, now I see it! Yes. How foolish of me! You look a lot like your brother, Stefano." (Pronounced: Stef-Faan-O.) She giggles, and when she does, a light blush flushes her cheeks. She stares down and into Marco's bright blue eyes. "Your brother said I should drop on by if I'm ever in New York, and well, here I am! Boy, and am I parched!"

He signals to Enzo. "Please, may I get you something from the bar?" Enzo waits.

"I hate drinking alone, will you join me?"

"Of course signora, of course..." Marco begins to speak Italian to his barman and friend, and soon Enzo is behind the bar doing what he does second best, tending bar. We'll leave his other more personal skills out of this. "I've taken the liberty of ordering for you a Gerardo.... My cousin's drink.... I hope you like it."

"I do like it. Your brother mixed one up for me, and I've been drinking them ever since...don't want to give you the wrong impression, but heck! I'm on vacation.... Now let's get down to business, 'cause this ain't no social call." She looks deep into his eyes, continuing, "...you sure look a lot like your brother.... It's uncanny!"

And they do look a lot alike; they could have been twins, if it weren't for the two years that separate them. They both have thick, steel-gray hair, though Stefano keeps his longer and in a ponytail. Both have blue eyes the color of the Adriatic, and both are short in stature. Both have pleasant broad faces that present a shadow of a beard soon after they shave. Although both Pollintini brothers practice that ritual every morning, sometimes Marco will take a shave at his barbershop on afternoons when business is slow. Both have a wide smile exposing dimples—on the left for Stefano, and on the right for Marco, but neither has dimples on both sides of his face. It's an anomaly rarely noticed or remarked upon; usually, Marco and his brother are standing together when it is, but Constance notices this right away, although she does not mention it.

"I'm looking to host a dinner for nine of my friends, and I'm hoping you can do it."

"Sure, Signora… we'd love to have you." He rises and takes a few steps to retrieve his book. "When would you like to come?"

"Tonight…. I know it's a short notice…. Dang—this whole trip has been an impulse! Tonight? Tonight at seven?"

"Signora, we're booked. I'm so sorry." They were booked. It wasn't a lie, or a ploy used to deter a request for a last-minute reservation. Marco has done that before, if he didn't need the business, or didn't like the attitude of the person making the request. He could jack up the cost, give his staff a workout, and everyone would make money. But today, he runs his finger down the page of names and numbers and looks up at Ms. Constance Cunningham and into her disappointment. She smiles, drops her long hand over Marco's, and looks into his expression with those large cow-brown eyes as he becomes physically uncomfortable from her touch. A cool bit of perspiration chills his neck, and Marco looks down upon her long fingers resting atop his wide hand. She glides her index finger across the cuff of his shirt, removes her hand, and lets out a sigh.

"My lady friends haven't all arrived yet," Constance says. "They're coming in from all over, and I promised them as real an Eye-talian meal as you could get in New York City. They'll be so disappointed. I know I should have called, but we really…." She pauses and takes a long sip of her drink. She pushes her Stetson back, freeing some of her auburn hair to fall across her forehead, and continues, "We really didn't think we'd actually pull this off. You see, I'm one of those Red Hat Ladies—you know?"

He didn't know. But now, as Constance Cunningham begins her explanation, Marco recalls once or twice seeing a group of ladies all in red hats

14

and dressed in purple walking around town. He had thought they were in a show or a circus, for who would choose to look so garish? She recites the short poem "Warning," by Jenny Joseph, and when he hears its contents, he laughs a bit at the attitude of the piece and chuckles a bit at her outfit. It all makes sense now and Marco, a man not easily charmed, is delighted by this woman and entertains the thought of opening the courtyard. The nights are getting warmer these days, he thinks, as he excuses himself to speak with his barman.

Constance cannot help noticing his wide back; from behind he looks like a Longhorn—sturdy, muscular. She is not used to short men: Her father, brothers, deceased husband Ed, and sons, Trevor and Will, were all well over six feet. Stefano was the shortest man she ever had relations with, and to be honest, outside of the two awkward boys she'd toyed with as a girl, Ed was the only real lover she'd had until Stefano. And Stefano was brief. Three days out of his six-day stay had been spent with Connie. She had just up and gone off with that Eye-talian, regardless of where the chips might fall. Her real friends had been envious of such a whirlwind romance. The others, the ones who gossiped, had been shocked, especially after her picture was posted in the Angelina Star, page 3, under the headline, "Local Socialite Entertains Italian Designer." Constance never read the article, but it had been filled with nasty insinuation. She did hear from both Trevor and Will. What was their remark? She thinks hard but is distracted by Marco and his employee speaking Italian. Stefano spoke Italian to her and although she knew not one single word, the sound made her weak and his intentional stare spoke a language she knew all too well. Stefano with his perceptions of the West, obtained mostly from film (some shot in Italy and Spain), is a loving memory for Constance. And at this point in her life, after being a daughter, wife, mother and grandmother, she feels very much like the woman in that poem she loves so.

She and Stefano at the Ritz in Dallas is a memory Constance cherishes and is not something of shame. That's it! She remembers now, Trevor on the phone, and then later, Will standing over her after she arrives home from Dallas, asking the exact same thing. "Aren't you ashamed of yourself?" It is the picture in the paper, and pictures are deceiving. They are dancing when it is taken and the stain is champagne that, jokingly, Stefano licks at, saying something like, "At $300 a bottle, you do not waste…" But the image is caught: Constance Cunningham with her large breasts, plunging neckline, diamond necklace, and head thrown back mid-laugh as Stefano wags his tongue far too close to her bosom. A picture like that should never be published; it is misleading and salacious. Now she remembers her response to both her sons, "Ashamed? Hell no!" And only to Will, who is far too pompous, she remembers saying, "Go shit in your hat, son. Maybe you'll release that stick you've had up there all these years!"

She drains her glass and pulls at the ends of her orange slice and eats it. She toys with the rind, plops it into the empty glass, and wipes her hands on the bar napkin. Her smile is wide as she hears that if she and her companions wouldn't mind dining outside on the courtyard, he, Marco himself, will cook for Constance and her guests. It is a courtesy to his brother's friend from the great state of Texas. Constance Cunningham respects Marco Pollintini's personal space by not hugging him, but she doesn't stop herself from admitting that she'd like to. At that point he says, "Bella… Bella," lifts her hand and kisses it. This is the first time her hand is ever kissed, and it is an act she always thought of as a silly, Hollywood gesture. It now becomes real, a tender moment making Constance blush, and it will live on in memory.

Marco explains the details of her dinner and for a fair price offers her a five-course traditional Italian meal (bar excluded), and she does not bat an eye at the price. She is a woman of means, and money talk ought to be handled in a businesslike manner, which it is, and although Marco has not told her the menu, he promises that she and her friends will be transported "to my home country, if only for the night. Tonight at 8:30, we will meet again, signora." Once again he lifts her hand, seems to breathe in her scent, and kisses her fingers. The tiny hairs at the back of his neck raise and once again, a tiny bit of perspiration cools his collar, reminding him that Constance Cunningham is a woman he'd like to know in a more intimate way.

Jules, the chef, and Marco meet to discuss logistics and the special menu for the ladies in the red hats. Marco has been left in complete control over it, including wine and cocktails, and Constance Cunningham couldn't have been happier. He could tell by the delight in her expression and the quickness of her step as she left the restaurant. He will start the ladies off with a Gerardo, their signature drink. The little bit of Campari mixed with vodka, soda, and fresh orange activates digestive juices and readies the stomach for that at which Marco Pollintini excels: a meal whose elements form a concerto that flows over one's palate the way music rushes over ones soul.

The Red Hat Lady Menu

Grilled Shrimp Wrapped in Crispy Pancetta

—

Pesto Linguini with Pan-Roasted Grape Tomatoes and Toasted Pine Nuts

—

Hearts of Celery Salad with Assorted House Cured Olives

—

Filet of Beef topped with White Truffle Butter, Sautéed
Spicy Spinach, and Roasted Garlic Toast

—

Lavender Panna Cotta Topped with a Single Red Raspberry
Floating on Raspberry Coulis

Everything on the menu could be easily made by the restaurant staff with the exception of the panna cotta. This is Marco's own creation in honor of the Red Hat Ladies. He will make this himself, and he needs to go to a special confectioner for the candied violets that will float upon the raspberry coulis. He hopes Constance will enjoy this extra touch. After his meeting with Jules, he has a brief conversation, all in Italian, with his trusted barman Enzo, the subject of which is not for public consumption. Then he speaks with Amy, who is to contact Sophia from Flowers-N-Such and is to decorate and ready the courtyard using only red, purple, and white. All the chargers must have a single white rose for each of the ladies lying on top of the printed menu. For some reason, unbeknownst to Marco, Amy seems giddy with the added work. "I have a feeling, just a feeling that this is going to be one helluva night, Mr. Pollintini!" She gets right on the phone and Marco thinks, *So far, it's been one helluva morning, why not one helluva night?*

At the height of lunch hour, Marco greets his regular customers and their guests with his usual charm. He pulls chairs for ladies, shakes hands with gentlemen, and directs his staff with the exactitude of a captain commandeering a ship through narrow straits. Restaurants run well have a rhythm all their own. After 2:00 p.m. Marco slips away from the helm to boil the cream for the panna cotta. He hums all the while, and the pastry chef, who is a bit put out when Marco gives her some free time so he can use her station, huffs as she heads out for an hour. Zennia will get over it. After all, it is his kitchen. The essence of lavender is such that if too much is used, the cream will be too perfume-y and, for Marco, inedible. Marco couldn't take any chances. Zennia is a great pastry chef, but at times she likes to knock it up a notch and could be a bit heavy with a subtle dessert like this one.

With his creative contribution out of the way, Marco decides to treat himself to a trim and shave at his barber before going home for a shower and change of clothes. That is forty minutes of alone time. True, he is at the barber's, and there are other men there with constant conversation, but Marco easily blocks out the chatter. Besides, Sal, his barber of twenty years, just knows when to be brief with the chitchat; it's the beauty of the place. Under the moist, hot towel, Marco turns his thoughts to Constance. He sees her in his mind's eye, but not in that awful dress. Here in the privacy of his head, she wears the red hat and tooled red boots, but instead of that mess of a dress, she is clad in a purple lacy bra, panties, black stockings, and, on her left leg, a bright red garter. This vision excites Marco, and under the barber smock, he relaxes into the moment and enjoys this image.

Constance has much to do before the rest of the ladies arrive. She flew in last night, and there are things she wants to do before the Red Hat Ladies gather at her suite. All her plans—the museum, her walk through St. Patrick's, her stop at Henri Bendel for a quick look-see—blow away like the dust of a summer storm upon leaving the restaurant. She keeps seeing that dimple on Marco's face as he smiles within her head. She sees his crystalline blue eyes and that mop of silver hair, and her thoughts stray back to his brother. Just how similar are the Pollintini brothers? A bit of city soot blows toward her face, and as she wipes at it, there is the faintest hint of citrus (his cologne), reminding her of that short man with the wide back. She remembers a different aroma under the scent she breathed in while her hand was atop his, and as she wipes at her cheek, she cannot help being pleasantly excited by the scent-memory of this Eye-talian.

Before she is truly aware of it, she is walking with the crowd toward, and then up, Fifth Avenue. The last time she felt so wistfully free was when she was with Stefano in Dallas. She knows the ladies will have a lot to say when they realize just who Marco is. They've all seen the picture in the Angelina Star. She herself posted it on the web so the other Red Hat Ladies could see what those small-minded Texans find so offensive. This is why she loves the ladies from her chat room: they do not judge. If anything, they encourage.... In fact—Christ!—Edith keeps posting that Connie should fly over to Milan and reignite that flame that still burns; it's just not as hot these days.

Is it fate, or just coincidence? She thinks, as she walks into Victoria's Secret, wondering if they even make dainties for women with fuller figures. The looks from the salesgirls are significant, and then she remembers her get-up. She sees herself in the long mirror, and although she likes what she sees, she recognizes that for New York, the whole costume needs to go. As luck would have it, a pretty, thin salesgirl with long legs, speaking in a Texas twang, gushes over her hand-tooled boots and red Stetson. Amber Kitteridge knows of the Red Hat Ladies; both her Mom and her Nana are members down in El Paso. She is a great help to Constance. To repay this kindness, for making her feel less than the spectacle she is in this getup, Constance offers to take Amber out for lunch. Amber jumps at the chance to be with this friendly lady in a town where friendliness is as common as a blasphemer at a tent revival meeting.

They dine at a little place on Seventh Avenue where the pizza is divine. Constance has but one slice and a small Coke while Amber has two—one plain, the other with the works—and a large root beer. For a skinny thing, she sure eats like a ranch hand.

"Come on to dinner tonight, honey." Constance is persuasive, but Amber will have none of it.

"I couldn't. I haven't earned the right. I haven't lived enough. I don't... it just seems disrespectful."

"Nonsense! Why, honey, it's just dinner. Besides, you don't have to dress up in purple and red."

"Really, Ms.—er—" Amber remembers Constance's insistence that they eschew such formality, "Connie, I'd rather not..."

And Constance Cunningham knows when to stop. Before they leave each other's company, they give each other a hug, as if they are old friends. Amber directs Constance to a crazy hat shop over by St. Mark's Place called MILLIE-Ners. The designer, Mildred Mowry, is a hip, middle-aged woman, who quit her corporate executive job a few years back and is now designing hats. Most are used as costumes for the theater or as accent pieces for the well-to-do ladies of New York City. Millie charges a fortune for her one- or two-of-a-kind creations, but they do make a statement: Art can and should be worn!

It proves difficult for Constance to find the place on her own. She is about to forgo a new hat. But each time she sees her reflection, she thinks it is time to lose this singin'-cowgirl look and find something different to wear. Lost in thought, she goes crosstown like a confused steer in a herd and miraculously finds St. Mark's Place.

Amid the tattoo/piercing parlors, T-shirt shops and cafes is the hat shop. Three faceless white mannequin busts, each on a rotating pedestal of different height, are on display in the window. Constance likes what she sees. The one on the left is a beaded beret that sparkles with iridescent crystals, and she thinks it must be heavy (it is not). The one on the right is completely made of feathers, and Constance is not sure whether they are natural or dyed, but the color is a sublime shade of blue that shifts ever so slightly in intensity as it slowly rotates. The centerpiece (on the tallest pedestal) is a disc that surrounds the crown in such a way that it gives the illusion of being a halo, but it is not gold. Instead, it is made from tightly woven bamboo strips in alternating shades of baby pink and yellow, making a geometric swirl subtle in appearance but complicated in its construction.

A pleasant chime sounds as she opens the door to enter the shop. There are other hats—all unique, all pieces of art. She spies her reflection in the large oval mirror that sits on the shop counter and cringes at her Annie Oakley getup. Millie herself, not the salesgirl in a white top hat, is quick to greet Constance. "That hat!" she proclaims, and Constance is ready for a verbal assault. Why wouldn't she be? Here is some New York hat designer about to denigrate her Stetson, which Connie had decorated herself. Connie added the feathers and band before she came to New York. Her discomfort makes her want to rush out of the shop and into the oncoming traffic. "May I see it?"

Constance removes it and hands it over, allowing her piled-up hair to fall about her shoulders, and watches as Mildred Mowry inspects her Stetson.

Mildred is a short woman with a round face. Her body is indiscernible under the black smock she wears. The smock acts as a workstation for Mildred: There are ribbons, pins, beads, and assorted threads sticking out of it. Constance can feel the criticism coming and begins to make excuses for her Patsy Cline appearance. But Mildred forestalls her, still examining the hat. "Please, madam...You look lovely! I like the embroidery...beautiful work...lovely. But the hat—did you buy this here, in town?"

"No." This woman gushes over her hat in such a way that Constance feels a pang of guilt for entertaining negative thoughts. Her mind is assuming far too much regarding this eccentric character. Funny thing: Mildred has immediately felt drawn to Constance because she perceives a fellow eccentric. Mildred knows very well of the Red Hat Ladies but can't remember ever having sold a hat to one of them. It isn't often she'll use red, and she remarks that it is not one of the colors she chooses first. "May I try it on?" she asks. Constance gives her permission with a gesture and a smile. The Stetson is a perfect fit. Mildred pushes it back off her forehead and admires herself in the mirror. Constance admits that the hat looks better on Mildred. "Really?" Mildred asks, turning to the left, and then to the right. "I love things Western. I've always wanted a Stetson and promised myself to get one, one day."

Soon Connie is chatting away about her dinner tonight with her friends and admits that she was thinking of ditching the Stetson for something less down-home. Mildred, still wearing the Stetson, asks if she will be wearing her Calamity Jane outfit tonight. It is not a malicious remark, and both ladies chuckle. The counter girl asks, "Who is Clammity Jane?" and both women chuckle louder.

Constance Cunningham describes tonight's purple suede dress thusly: "The hides have been treated in such a way that it is as thin as finely woven Egyptian cotton. The color is a lighter shade of purple than this, but purple it is. Make no mistake about that! It has a full skirt and the bodice is constructed, almost like a sleeved corset. It has a stiff collar that does—" Here she points at her cleavage and with her index fingers shows the sweep of the collar around her neck. "It really is a simple thing, and yet not. I guess you'd have to see it."

Before Constance could stop it, both women are in a cab and heading over to the Parker-Meridian. Mildred still wears the Stetson. Soon they are in her suite, and as Constance pulls the dress bag from the closet, her phone begins to ring.

"Yes. No. Please meet me here at seven and don't be late. I have a car—more like a white tank—to drive us, and I do not want to be late. Yes…no…Marco's…" She snickers a bit and finishes her conversation with, "There's a terrace, so you know what to bring. Don't disappoint the girls." She places the phone back on its base and zips open the bag.

Mildred does more than look at the dress. She inspects it like a kindergarten teacher looking for nits. She fondles the suede with gentle care. "It has a retro look, right out of the Fifties and yet modern. The constructed bodice is art! The hints of red at the collar and sleeve are perfect…red satin throughout the skirt…lush! I love the three-quarter sleeve! And these buttons on the cuff and collar are divine, simply divine! The dress is fabulous!"

"They ought to be; they're pure Chilean garnets," Constance says. "And the dress—well, I gave Viv, the dressmaker back home, a tea dress my mother used to wear. I had it saved in tissue stored in the attic. That dress is light yellow chiffon; it has a sash at the waist with a big pink bow around the back. She patterned this dress after that old tea dress of Mother's, and I think she did a super job."

"Put it on." It is not a request. Upon seeing Constance in her dress, Mildred sighs and remarks that the dress is lovely.... "It is a dream of a dress! Stay here, use the spa, have a massage.... I'll be back." And just like that, Mildred Mowry leaves Constance Cunningham alone in her suite and flies out the door, still with the Stetson still upon her head.

Constance removes her new lingerie, which she'd put on with the dress, and fingers the delicate fabric. Without much thought she takes them into her bathroom and rinses them with tepid water and a drop or two of Woolite. They bleed a bit and after three rinses with cool water, she wraps them in a rolled towel to remove most of the wet. Her under garments hang to air dry and if they are still damp when she needs them—well, the room has a hair dryer; she'll just use that if she must.

By 5:00 p.m., after her mild work-out, steam, shower, sauna, and half-hour massage, Constance is ready for a quick bath and a cool drink. The ladies are due to arrive at seven. All but Edith have called to announce their arrival, and all are excited about tonight. Constance tries to call Marco to tell him that there may be another for dinner and is disappointed that he is not there to take her call. Amy assures her that one more for dinner will be fine and she will take care of it. Connie is impressed by this young, pretty girl and the enthusiastic way in which she expresses herself.

Memory fuses with fantasy, and while in the tub, Constance is overcome by carnal thoughts that decent women just do not utter.... ever! But here in her mind's eye, she can see things that make her ache in a way that no doctor could cure. Unless that doctor looked like a Pollintini brother, and his cure is a good, long, steady, determined plowing, as of a fallow field in spring, she thinks. She connects no guilt to these thoughts, and when the remonstrations of her two sons make a show, Connie pushes away those thoughts with an audible, "Bullshit!"

She does need to blow-dry her undies, mostly the bra, but soon they are bone-dry and soft to the touch. Connie looks at herself in the mirrored closet doors and likes what she sees. For a woman her age, she is curvy in all the right places. Covering herself in a lavender full slip, she remembers Elizabeth Taylor in *Cat on a Hot Tin Roof*, although Elizabeth's slip was the palest cream. The phone rings announcing one of her guests. It is just 6:30, and whoever it is early and will have to endure Connie finishing her make-up and dressing. She orders three bottles of champagne, all on ice and in buckets, and while waiting for the first guest, wraps herself up in the plush, white robe provided by the hotel. The buzz at the door has her rushing to embrace a friend she knows only from the web and from two other Red Hat Lady dinners. Instead, she is surprised to see her very own Stetson, and under it, Mildred Mowry, holding a black hat box with "MILLIE-Ners" scripted in hot pink across the top.

"I've been wondering when you'd be back," Constance says, and then asks a silly question: "What's in the box?" But the box remains closed. "Never mind the box- what are you going to do with your hair?" Connie looks to her reflection Millie is already picking at Connie's mop of hair, and soon is styling it with the brushes and combs that lie on the mirrored vanity. By pinning it back and fluffing at her bangs, Millie creates a different look for Constance Cunningham. There is nothing relaxed about this hairstyle; it is elegant and cosmopolitan. "Now put on your dress before I let you see what's inside this box." A gentle knock raps on the suite's door; it is a waiter with the champagne, and Connie feels relief that the ladies are not here yet. The gentleman is quietly professional as he sets the table, pops the first bottle, and readies the table with glasses from the kitchen area of her suite. After he pours two flutes for the ladies present, he is sent away with his tip.

"Luscious... simply luscious!" Mildred takes a step back as Connie slowly turns like one of those mannequin pedestals at MILLIE-Ners. The suede is surprisingly fluid. It moves like jersey, or a man-made material. "Let me see the shoes."

"I was going to wear the boots. They were made special for me, and I think they're the only hand-crafted Eye-talian cowboy boots on the planet. But just last week, these came from Milan..." She goes to the shoe bag that rests on a hook in her closet and removes a swath of gray flannel. They are a simple woman's flat shoe with just an insinuation of a heel. What makes them unique are the color—Chinese red, with beadwork at the top of the shoe in a stunning Native American starburst of purple and white. Mildred audibly gasps when she sees them.

"They're beautiful..." She touches the leather and likes the feel. "Wherever did you get them?"

"Stefano made them for me," Connie explains. "To be honest, I thought he was a bit of a 'per-vert' when he made a cast of my feet. I thought, *God! Whatever would he want that for?* But I let him, and a month after his visit, my boots came. I called him to thank him. Sent him a complete John Wayne Western collection of DVDs—he loves the Westerns, you know. And I told him me and the girls were coming to New York for a get-together. Then, these came. He knew I was dressing up, and wanted me to have these; made them special, just for me."

"Stefano? I thought he only made shoes for men?"

"Are you ever going to show me what is in that box?" Constance drinks her first flute and pours herself another, as Mildred sips from her own, and then deposits it on the vanity and opens the box. In the mirror, Connie sees the back of Mildred and a flurry of pink tissue paper. The champagne makes her giddy with Christmas morning excitement; she feels just like a child! Mildred turns with her creation lying atop her upturned hands. It is a simple pillbox hat in the shape of a teardrop; coincidentally, it is of a shade quite similar to the shoes. At its point is an amethyst pin fastening a tiny bunch of lavender silk cornflowers.

"You made this?"

"Just for you, dear."

"What do I owe you? I'm in shock! It's beautiful." Mildred places the hat upon Connie's head, and attaches it with two hatpins, that are hidden by her hair.

Now it is Mildred's turn to finish her first flute and replenish her glass with the bubbling deliciousness. While Connie is admiring her reflection, Mildred says, "Nothing…Well, nothing in cash. I want your Stetson."

"That was already yours, dear. Join us for dinner, please. Besides, the restaurant expects you…. There's an extra seat."

Mildred accepts, and soon the suite is filled with the Red Hat Ladies, giggling, drinking, and gushing over Constance's dress, hat, and shoes. By far, Constance has outdone this coterie of eccentrics with her outfit, Millie thinks. Millie herself fits in wonderfully with her purple camisole, jeans, and large, red Stetson. Doris and Samantha, from Saddle River, New Jersey, drove in this morning and are staying at the Warwick. Both are in purple suits by Chanel: Doris in plaid, and Sam in tight, multi-colored tweed. Millie pronounces their hats "sweet." Doris sports a red fedora with matching plaid band, and Sam has the exact same fedora with no band, but instead, a diamond dragonfly pin, attaching long purple and red feathers.

As each woman arrives, Millie boldly introduces herself and becomes fast friends and is soon chatting with them as if they had all been friends for years. When she learns that the women's friendships developed over the web, she is simply amazed.

Mary wears a purple tuxedo that she rented.... "I had to go all the way to Lexington, Kentucky," she says. The red top hat was even harder to find. With her slim figure and cropped hair, she could pass for a man, except for the hands; Millie notices her long slender digits with envy. There is a piano in the suite, and Mary sits at it and plays while they wait for the car.

Nancy has come very close to outdoing Constance. She arrives clad in a floor-length purple cape lined in red silk. It closes at the neck with a large brocade gold latch-button, thick and dramatic. She has red feathers in her hair, but when she removes the cape, under it is a simple purple dress. It is neat and elegant, yet incongruous with her feathery head. Darlene and Lisa both wear purple raw silk blouses and black pants they got at Filene's. On their heads are purple berets embellished with bright red glass beads. "We sewed the beads on ourselves, but they weigh a ton!" Lisa confides to Millie. Kate wears a simple A-line dress that is more lavender than purple, with a dark pink cloche adorned by an enamel ladybug pin. It is a sweet, girlish look. Jen looks like a pretty transvestite, Millie thinks. She wears a slinky vintage Halston purple halter gown and a bright red ostrich feather jacket. Millie likes what she sees. There is much laughter and chatting.... They sip their champagne and order two more bottles. These ladies enjoy their bubbly.

"Where's Edith?" Constance asks.

"She's meeting us at Marco's," Darlene says. "She got in late. Mike wouldn't let her fly up, so he drove her, dropped her off at the Waldorf, and went out to Long Island to fish. She was so angry. I had to calm her down over the phone and promised her that I'd bring the weed I had to get my daughter's boyfriend, Trent, to get me some, and he assures me it's excellent." Darlene waves her purse. She and Lisa make their way toward the balcony, and soon a waft of pungent smoke floats into the suite.

"You…ladies, will you ever grow up?" Doris is adamant that she will not partake, but every other lady present goes out upon the balcony to smoke pot. Millie can smell the thick aroma over the mixture of perfumes that invade the suite. Although she has never smoked a cigarette, she tries it, coughs a great deal, and says she feels nothing. However, the champagne has made her a bit light-headed, and as soon as she wonders vacantly about the car, the telephone rings to announce its arrival.

The night air refreshes the ladies, who are seemingly oblivious to the looks and possible comments from onlookers. They are a spectacle—that is certain. *But they are all about fun,* Millie thinks. The ride to Marco's is long for a New Yorker who is used to walking almost everywhere. But the chatter and overall camaraderie of these women delights Millie. Through the impact of a poem the medium of the web, these women are now important parts of each other's lives.

Marco himself is there to greet his special guests. He and Edith are waiting outside when the ostentatious oversized vehicle pulls up to the restaurant. Edith is most tastefully dressed: black pencil skirt to accentuate her lithe legs, crisp white man-tailored shirt, a narrow black tie, and over it a plum cardigan of the lightest weave. On her head is a raspberry beret, and Millie thinks of a song by Prince with that very name. As she takes in this scene, her mind drifts a bit, and Millie now thinks those few puffs on the balcony are making her mind flit from this to that, from here to there. She likes it.

Nick, the limo driver, is quick to open the door and usher the ladies out of the car. There are squeals, hugs, and kisses between Edith and each passenger. It is Marco, however, who greets Constance at the car door, to take her hand and lead them, like a procession, through the restaurant toward the courtyard. Amy holds the door as they pass, greeting them with a cordial, "Welcome to Marco's," and smiles an extra bit as Marco, clad in pressed kitchen whites with no toque upon his head, escorts Ms. Cunningham out, onto the courtyard. A few patrons stand to get a clearer view of Marco parading this purple party through the bar.

Tiny white lights sparkle above the dining table. A low, long arrangement of white spider mums, crimson roses, and feathery purple liatris decorates the table. Marco had Amy print out the poem, "Warning," on decorated paper as a cover for the menu. It will be a memento of their visit to Marco's. Atop each menu is a single white rose. The women ooh and aah over the courtyard. "How lovely; it's magical. Oh, Constance it's wonderful!" Constance gently squeezes Marco's hand and smiles at him. He beams. .

Soon, Enzo's brother, Rob, makes his way through the group of ladies, offering drinks.

"This is delicious!"

"I don't care who Gerardo is, but I love his drink!"

"It's so refreshing…"

"It doesn't feel like a drink-drink!"

And as each course is served, so is a different, hand-selected wine. Marco knows that if his feelings for this strange woman were different, he would lean toward an unnecessarily expensive wine. After all, this is business. But for some strange reason, he feels toward this woman he just met the way he feels toward family. Another thing that simmers within Marco's brain is his physical attraction to the lady in that cowgirl outfit. Now she looks like a great lady. She is elegant, chic, and yet, underneath, a fiery whole woman who knows how to love and be loved. He watches her among her friends, not only when he appears at the beginning and end of each course, but also surreptitiously from his office window.

"Pancetta? I never had that before…scrumptious!" It would be rude to express what Marco thinks as he looks at Darlene and Lisa smacking their lips.

"The perfect amount of pasta—not too little, and not too much."

"Roasted grape tomatoes…"

"Celery root? I must get Agnes, my cook, to get some."

"So refreshing…"

The main course arrives all at the same temperature, medium rare, and there is not one complaint. But there are numerous requests for another piece of roasted garlic toast. The ladies are all pleasantly enjoying themselves, and Amy, who has been dying to get out there just to witness at first hand some of the antics of what she calls these "fun, *fun* ladies," gets to take their beverage order. Rob stands close by so there are no mistakes. These people, he thinks, must be special. Rob has worked Marco's before, and this has never happened. Nor, according to Amy, has Marco been so pleasantly demanding of the kitchen and house staff.

The night is a resounding success. Constance stands next to Marco sipping her Sambuca and now notices his constant pawing of the Belgian block under their feet. Right, and then left, scratching the surface like a bull about to charge. When she looks down, she sees that hers are not the only shoes with adornments. Marco wears silver tipped cowboy boots. Before she has a chance to remark, Marco explains that they're new and he does not want to slip.

"Stefano?"

"But of course, signora, he is my brother. I did not know he was making boots so…American. Actually, on my way home, between shifts, I was thinking that those boots of yours were probably a gift from my brother, right?" She nods and smiles. "I didn't think at first, but when I got home, these were there with a note: 'Fratello…er, Brother, I thought you might like these. Stefano.' That was it. They're beautiful, no?" He lifts his pant leg, and just like her very own they are stunning, uniquely Stefano and yet classically American.

"The hides are mine, I think," says Constance. "We've been doing business…. Actually, my son, Will, ships calfskins, and in season, doeskins to Milan. According to Will, business with your brother is good." She isn't about to divulge Will's rather stern opinion about her own dealings with Marco's brother. Will, will always be just like his father: narrow-minded.

Rob brings the coffees and Amy wheels out the panne cotte. Ten little plates in a circle surround a purple mannequin head, similar to the ones at Mildred's. And on top, a red hat, fashioned out of marzipan, replete with white chocolate doves, which are clutching edible miniature sugary purple grapes. Mildred is in awe. Marco, who sprang for the creation, brings out Zennia, who created it, to a round of jubilant applause. Giving her a creative challenge is his way of making up to his pastry chef for taking over her station earlier. She bitched at first, as is her way, but when he returned and saw what she was able to do in such a brief time, he knew she was golden. *I might have to give her a raise, soon,* he thinks, as Zennia beams at the ladies.

Doris stops Rob from serving, and all the ladies, except Constance, begin clicking their cameras, setting up poses with Zennia and shots of different clusters of ladies around the dessert. Then Amy and Zennia use all the ladies' cameras and camera-phones to capture the whole group with Constance at the center. Now Constance insists upon a picture of just herself and Marco, and all the ladies oblige. Constance leans against this boulder of a man, looks down into his eyes, and says, "This is lovely." He takes her hand gently into his own, and she tickles his palm as her fingers become engulfed by his meaty paw. The image is a classic bride and groom pose with this exception: The groom looks up into the loving eyes of his bride, and not the other way around. Even with her low-heeled shoes and his cowboy boots, Constance still towers over Marco Pollintini.

Soon, she is back at her place, tasting the lightest of desserts. Truly unique, it is something Constance has never tasted before.

"Lavender.... Who would have thunk it?" Sam murmurs as she lovingly licks at her spoon.

"These flowers—I thought they were real! They're sugar and just melt in your mouth! I want another," Edith comments to no one in particular.

They sip at the assorted liqueurs and coffees, all the while savoring Marco's gesture of love. He leaves, comes back to check on them, and finds them sharing a marijuana cigarette. Two of the women were smoking cigarettes, which is allowed, but never marijuana. Amy sniffs at the air, giggles, and would love nothing more than to grab a cappuccino and an extra panna cotta and join these women. She whispers in Marco's ear that it'll be over soon, and not to make a big deal of something so minor. His reply is a stern, "Get to your station." As she leaves, she turns before entering the bar, and he winks at her, exposing that dimple on the right side of his cheek. Marco's look toward Ms. Cunningham does not include the wink, but the dimple is in full view.

Mildred is organizing the rest of the evening. "I'm hosting an after-party, party at my place. Please, all of you, let's go. There's a club nearby—real Chi-Chi, you know! I'm very close with the landlord, so I'm always on the list." Mildred is firm: They must all come, see her shop, smoke some more of those funny cigarettes, and possibly go dancing.

"Mike will kill me!" Edith proclaims and giggles a bit as Sam, Doris and Darlene recite "Warning." The others join in, but some need to use the printed page so lovingly made by that sweet girl, Amy.

"Girls…" Constance stands and, with the last sip of her Sambuca, toasts Marco and his "marvelous staff. Never have I felt so welcomed: Never have we been treated so well. *Cent'anni:* A hundred years of health and happiness to you, Marco Pollintini." But he hears: "Chain-donny" and "Poll-in-teeeni," and is charmed.

"Wait…" he shouts, raises a hand, utters something in Italian that only Millie understands, "…I need a drink. Or it is not a toast." Enzo appears with a shot of grappa for his boss. Marco nods, Enzo disappears, and the ladies all utter some bastardization of *"Cent'anni."* Now, it is Marco who raises his glass toward the table, but specifically to Constance. "It has been our pleasure to serve such elegant and stylish ladies." They all look at each other's costume—for that is what each of them is wearing, a costume—laugh a bit, and consume the last drop of their after-dinner drink.

Constance has the car wait outside, while Mildred prods her new friends onward, toward the garish Texas-large vehicle. Tugging at Mildred's arm, she says, "Go ahead without me. I'll meet you there. I've got to settle the bill."

"Go to the black door to the right of the shop, and ring the buzzer." Constance nods with understanding as Millie herds the Red Hat Ladies into the car. "Wait until we get to my place for that. You don't want to make Nick all screwy while he drives!" Constance chuckles, hearing both Sam and Doris shout out, "There's a window between us and him!" The door slams as the monster-vehicle lumbers its way into the city traffic.

As she reenters the restaurant, Constance can see a flurry of activity outside on the courtyard. Short men, familiar to her by their thick raven hair, are busy cleaning and readying the restaurant for the next day's business. Had they been there so long that Marco's is ready to close? The time on Amy's wristwatch, excessively large for such a thin wrist, reads 12:20. This saddens her a bit, but knowing everything has an end, she enters the bar where Enzo awaits her.

"Beautiful lady, Marco needed to do some things in the office. We will settle up and if you don't mind, Mr. Pollintini would like you to stay a bit, until he returns."

Enzo is charming. Amy is a delight. Bypassing Enzo, she offers Connie a drink, to practice her skill at mixology. Enzo and she exchange a light banter in Italian. "I really shouldn't," says Connie, irresolutely. But as she examines the bill, with her glasses on (it seems incredibly reasonable), she waves her hand and says that she'll have a piña colada, providing there are two straws, "...so we could share it." Connie hands Enzo her Amex card, putting the whole thing on her corporate account. Trevor will just have to deal with it.

Amy goes to work, and Enzo cannot stop himself from teasing her, all in Italian. Amy begins rattling off a fluid, foreign response. By her tone and expressive gestures, it can't be pleasant, yet, it is music for Connie; charming, mellifluous music.

"Hey...d'jou kiss you *mother* with that mouth?"

Amy's response is so fast and fiery that Enzo chuckles, looks to Constance, "Ah, signora, the face of an angel and the mouth of Satan himself. I would be embarrassed to repeat to you, a lady, what that *strega nella travestimento*...excuse me...a witch...a witch with a false face...."

"A disguise, you Italian weasel. Enzo, you've been here 20 years, why isn't your English any better?"

Now the river of Italian exclamations comes from Enzo. Again, it is wonderfully musical and comical to the lady from Texas. "Chain-donny!" Constance sips at the piña colada through a straw, and both Enzo and Amy are too polite to laugh. Enzo runs the card at the end of the bar while she and Amy taste the luscious drink. Amy chatters, recounting the stir in the restaurant when the Red Hat Ladies paraded out onto the courtyard. She gushes over the suede dress and asks to touch its supple texture. "To be honest, it's a bit heavy to wear, but it was worth it. I might wear it again, someday." Soon, the drink is half empty, Enzo is gone, and Amy seems anxious.

"You got something, lady. Mr. Pollintini never wears whites. Not as long as I've been here, and he rarely sets up such a special menu...for anyone. Usually, he just lets the cook handle everything, but after you left, I don't know. Today was just different."

Connie smiles, sips then looks up at the doorway where Marco Pollintini, no longer dressed in his whites, but clad in a sharkskin suit that shines from the overhead lighting. Beneath it he wears a purple shirt and deep red tie. Marco stands looking and listening into his bar. On his feet are the boots with the silver adornments. He becomes more appealing every time she sees him, Connie thinks. She was attracted to him this afternoon, but now— now her head swims from memory. As he sidles up to her, she thinks the drink and that little bit of pot just might make her vulnerable to a man so appealing.

"Signora…Amy…." He smiles, exposing his dimple, and Amy and Enzo are soon on their way to get their coats and leave Marco's, a bit earlier than usual. As they say goodnight, Constance stands and taking a few crisp bills from her purse, hands them to Enzo, telling him to share them with Amy, "and anyone else who spent extra time today making my gathering a success." He tries to hand the money back, but Constance will not hear of it.

"Thank you…Madonna," and just as Marco did earlier, Enzo takes her hand and kisses it. It does not have the same effect, but it charms Constance and she kisses him lightly on both cheeks.

———

Table 64 sits at the rear of Marco's Italian Restaurant. It is large and seats eight or ten persons upon the banquette that curves behind the table. The fabric is man-made, durable, suede. It is gray and cleans remarkably well. Table 64 is usually unoccupied. The diners at Marco's rarely exceed six to a party; it is a place for more intimate gatherings. Constance hears a series of tweets and beeps as Enzo sets the alarm. Marco gently places his hand in hers and leads her away from her piña colada, which she is growing tired of anyway. Table 64, she notices, is the only one with a flickering candle. It is the only one set. As they draw near she takes in the sight: a crystal decanter with a deep amber fluid in it, two small plates, sliced bread, miniature pears, and a platter of cheese.

"You would think that I couldn't eat another thing, and yet…this is so tempting," she exclaims. He describes each of the four cheeses, names the specific regions they come from, and briefly tells the process by which they are made. He pours very old port (Spanish, he tells her, nodding to the

33

excellence of the product) into delicate glasses and makes for Constance a sampler a cheeses and a bit of sliced Seckel pear. She sips, nibbles and listens while Marco drifts from food to history, saying how this building that he now owns was once a speakeasy in the Twenties. He rises, starts moving chairs about, and slides the table closest to table 64 away from where she sits. He returns, smiling all the while.

They sit close. "Now watch this…. I've only shown this to five other people: Enzo, my brother, and some workmen I trust." She doesn't see how he does it, but the table glides away from them, exposing a second floor. When the table stops, Constance notices a large brass latch. Marco stands and lifts the latch, and from beneath, an inviting glow emerges from the floor. "Come…. Don't be afraid."

Afraid? Constance was only afraid once in her adult life. That was when her boy, Will, was thrown from that nasty horse of her husband's. The doctors never thought he'd recover; that frightened her. Seeing where old gangsters hid their hooch is nothing that Constance fears. And although she just met Marco, she knows that there is nothing to fear from this well-dressed Eye-talian as he descends the circular staircase. Here is a perfect opportunity for him to look up her full skirt, but like a gentleman, he turns his gaze away and returns only when he hears her shoe hit the red brick that covers the floor.

"I was going to knock through that wall and make this all the wine cellar, but the building wouldn't be able to take it. Our wine cellar is on the other side of that wall. I've had three engineers, and they all agree: It should not be done." She scans the room and sees that it is decorated with expensive paintings and it looks like a salon from the Belle Époque. A deep crimson velvet curtain hides the stone wall. Something just may be behind it, Connie thinks, and she doesn't much care. The sconces on the wall, once fueled by gas, have been adapted to deliver a soft electric light that casts shadows about this secret room. She examines one painting, and sees a masterpiece by some Italian from the Renaissance. The subject is a bacchanal. Bare-breasted women are ravished by burly men in olive branch crowns, and Pan is piping his flute on a rock, pleasurably looking down upon men reclined into and onto willing women. The whole scene is bathed in a lush, golden light. Marco is behind her. She feels his heat, turns, and without a word, they kiss. The air is rich with age and scented by a large bouquet of purple and red roses that sit on a low table next to a sofa of gray suede. She knows he's done this before, and as with the question of what's behind the thick curtain, doesn't care. They are in each other's arms, and it is ecstasy.

Constance thinks briefly about Stefano and his boyish approach to love-making: fast, electric and filled with laughter throughout. Marco is deliberate. He is serious with the power and determination of—well, a bull, she thinks; a pleasant, pleasing bull, with a strong back, but deft and gentle as he undresses her. A deep guttural vibration emanates from his throat between whispers of "Bella, bella," as her breathing becomes rhythmic from his touch. She sprawls across the couch much in the same way as one of those lusty ladies in the painting, only she is in purple and red undergarments from Victoria's Secret.

Marco cannot believe his eyes as his daylong fantasy plays out before him. He can't stop whispering and muttering in his native tongue. He knows what this will do to this vulnerable lady; knows that for some, a foreign tongue is an aphrodisiac. He removes his boots and places them under the table. Marco takes his time removing his suit and leaves only his black boxers on as he sits and looks into Constance's waiting stare. Her ebony eyes bounce light back into his eyes, and he feels a connection deeper than he has ever known. Soon, his massive fingers are all over her. He toys with the lacy bra, and before he can undo the clasp between her breasts, it pops and he buries his face there.

Constance writhes under his weight and matches his every motion with one of her own. Time, space, dead husbands, remonstrative sons, business, her past, those friends with the purple dresses and red hats—all are gone. In this all-too-short moment, she is nothing and everything. She becomes a part of a man she barely knows, and feels whole.

Marco's eyes roll in the back of his head more than once, his pleasure is so great. There had been many women in Marco's life, but none like this. For him, Constance is deliciously alien. Her size, her organic willingness to please and be pleased by him, has Marco more potent than his usual self, and he is wildly matching her every twist and undulation of her full figure.

Going back to Texas will be difficult. It is a good thing she is a woman of means and can travel, she thinks, as they lay wrapped in each other's arms. Marco is like a furnace, his frame exudes a heat, and she is calm in their mutual embrace. They make love a second time and it is longer and surprisingly more pleasurable than the first.

Behind the curtain was a narrow door, through which was a small bathroom and shower. There were large, freshly laundered white terry towels and robes with matching slippers. Constance wonders how he knew that he'd be entertaining. Once again, she discovers that she doesn't give a flying cow patty.

They shower together in the tiny stall and wash each other with genuine interest and care. It is more than sensuous. It is deeper. It is tender. It is sublime. They towel dry each other and tend to themselves only after a kiss. Both are humming, unaware that neither is humming the same tune.

As they make their way back up and into the restaurant, Marco now has no compunction against sliding his hand up her red-lined skirt and pinching her lace-encased ass. She giggles like a schoolgirl and calls him "Gigolo," and he pulls her toward him with a deep stare. Marco tells her something that makes her melt into his embrace like cotton candy on the tongue. "Signora, if I were a gigolo; I'd be a poor one at that…. My devotion to you would be too strong to ever stray like those loose, immoral men. If I could paint, you would be my only subject…. If I were a poet, reams of pages would be devoted to your beauty and my deep yearning…. You are a goddess."

"Stop! My God! You Eye-talians are too much. Just, too, too much!"

Constance never joins her friends at Mildred's that evening. Later, however, she does read numerous posts from all nine of them online. She missed quite the night. Mike refuses to speak to Edith, even left her for a week to cool off, after that picture in the *New York Post*—on the cover, no less! At least Constance had the decency to be on page three. Besides, Connie would never strike a policeman, no matter what!

Millie and she are now close. Constance stays with Millie during the wait for marriage license necessities. Trevor is skeptical, and Will refuses to come to the wedding, saying that his mother has lost her mind. What was it he said? Especially after she told him who Marco is…. "One Eye-talian wasn't enough for you? You went after his brother? That's sick, Mom—'bout the sickest thing I ever did hear of. Besides, isn't that incest?" Constance is still surprised by her response. She began to recite "Warning" to her belligerent son, all the while thinking: "Go shit in your hat, son. Maybe it'll remove that stick that's been up there…way too long!"

LI

I write of the wish that comes true—for some reason a terrifying concept.
—James M. Cain

I

Xin Peng is swollen. Not only is this baby far too big for her tiny frame, but for some reason (her doctor has yet to explain why) Xin cannot stop drinking that American drink Gatorade. Her cravings began shortly after her second trimester, and she just could not sate the urge. Orange being the desired flavor, Xin stocks her larder with those plastic bottles. As she reaches for her third one this morning, her contractions come painfully swift and hard. She knows what to do, but knowing that this baby is promised, contractually so, to an American family, Xin prays that if she could only keep it awhile longer, inside her the baby would remain hers.

She grips the small wooden table, bends, and squeezes her short legs together. There is no stopping this, and as she realizes this, her water breaks, wetting her inner thighs, ankles, and feet, and spreading a liquid shadow beneath her swollen frame. How she hates her husband at this moment. Xin wishes she could inflict on Hau this physical torture. Then, he would know the true pain of carrying and delivering a new life. But her real pain, the kind her money-hungry husband and father of her two children would never know, was the anguish that her child, this unnamed, baby girl, would never know her own mother.

During this pregnancy, moments of blissful forgetfulness had Xin fantasizing the bond between mother and daughter. She saw herself brushing a girl child's hair, teaching her music, watching her grow. Then the cold realization that this would never be would smack her, bringing with it a pain deeper than the pain she now feels as the baby tries to free itself from her womb.

She cries out for her son to get his father from the small shop at the far end of their village. She sits herself on the low stool she sometimes uses to keep her swollen ankles elevated. Her tears are unstoppable. No sobs. No whimpers. Only tears, slow and steady, stream from her ebony eyes. If she could only run and hide, have this baby in another town far from her avarice-driven husband. Keep it hidden until the little girl is too old for that American couple.

Why don't they adopt one of their own kind? She thinks. *Aren't there American children who need homes?* But Xin knows the answer. Americans are rich and money buys them anything they want. Even living Chinese dolls they can treat like exotic pets. And won't their friends be envious of their unique new toy? They will dress her in American clothes (probably made over here in Asia), teach her American ways, and make of Xin's only girl something ugly, something American.

That pain again. That twisting, pushing, and ripping pain makes Xin cry out again. Not for help though, not for relief. This pain has her scream out to the universe a wish: "Come back to me, little one. Do whatever you must, but come back to me. Make those Americans pay for your father's ugly sin. Make every waking moment of their lives full of regret and sorrow for their selfishness, and come back home to your mother!" She rolls off the stool onto her clean kitchen floor chanting her wish, cursing this unborn baby girl.

II

Jerri Lee is crying again. Her tears wet her chin as she pulls at her straight black hair. She drops to her knees, rolls to her side, gulps air, and slowly begins to fall asleep out of sheer exhaustion. Trudy Lawrence covers the child with a thin rag of a blanket that she had earlier thrown away and has since retrieved out of desperation. It smells of sour milk and is flecked with bits of dried crumbs from cookies eaten long ago. When Jerri was younger, the blanket, once pale yellow with a border of pink satin, was part of the weekly laundry. Now Trudy can't remember the last time she washed the damn thing and can no longer let Jerri Lee keep it, yet it did quiet her. The satin, torn and stringy from little Jerri sucking on its smoothness, no longer resembles the color pink. Dirty beige, she thinks, looking down on her troubled toddler. Strands of hair matted from tears lay across pudgy cheeks. Her bangs lie off to one side, her tiny nostrils flare to take in air, and her shut eyelids flicker slightly as Jerri's sleep takes on a less intense quality. The breaths become slower and more even until finally, her little face relaxes. She is sound asleep, or in this case, soundlessly asleep on the carpeted floor, and Trudy hopes it lasts at least an hour, or if she is lucky, maybe two.

Quietly and quite unconsciously, Trudy begins to hum a Disney tune. It seems to run through her head daily now. Once it would soothe her baby. Lately, though, it enrages her, and Trudy has evicted the tune from her repertoire of quieting lullabies. Now that the child sleeps, Trudy sings it low and makes herself a cup of herbal tea. After this morning and countless nights of disturbed rest, Trudy doubts the tea will soothe her, but the ritual may. She sings, "Baby mine, don't you cry. Baby mine, dry your eyes. Rest your head close in my arms..." But cry is all her baby o' mine does. Or, if she is not crying, she is destroying something. It's a phase, her developmental psychologist husband Dave says. For that very reason they must have patience and let their adopted baby girl express her emotions in a free environment. That is, if they want a well-rounded and emotionally healthy person to develop. But Dave isn't here as much as Trudy is, and Dave—Dr. Dave to all their friends—refuses to accept the fact that neither of them is cut out for child rearing.

The very first time Trudy held Jerri in her arms, the baby wailed, and it seems she has been crying for three straight years. Trudy tried rocking, humming, and out of desperation placing her dry teat near Jerri Lee's tiny pursed lips. She stopped the crying for less than a minute, and Trudy thought she had latched onto a temporary solution. The baby, however, realizing no comfort would ever come from this sagging middle-aged mammary, screeched all the more. She plopped the bundled baby in Dave's arms. The child quieted. Dave could soothe her. In Dave's arms the child cooed and slept. That was not to last long.

The long flight from China saw Trudy rocking in her belted seat trying to quiet the child, not only for herself and Dave but for the rest of the passengers on the flight. The looks and comments still live with her today. Trudy could not blame them. Being locked in the plane's cabin with a screaming infant was a nuisance, but there was something else. Her internal voice told Trudy that some of the women on board were actually harboring ill feelings toward this American couple for having an Asian baby in their clumsy arms.

Dave would probably say that she was being paranoid, being a nervous new mother, but Trudy knew her feelings were not creations of her mind.

One woman with an ancient face exchanged looks with her aisle mate, chatting frantically. Had the Lawrences understood Mandarin, they probably would have been on the next flight back to China to return this inconsolable infant. The woman closest to Trudy extended her arms and Trudy handed over her baby to this probable grandma. Her deep crevices stretched into a smile and as she spoke quietly to the baby, little Jerri Lee stopped her piteous crying and finally rested in the arms of a stranger. And here, on their very flight home from China, was where Trudy's resentment of Dave began. In his most condescending, sing-song voice, the voice he used on some of his more petulant patients, he said, "Trudy, you know, now that Jerri Lee is ours—well, you're going to have to soothe her and comfort her during this transition." He talked on about the dynamics of a mother-daughter bond, and Trudy heard none of it. All Trudy heard was, "Now that Jerri Lee is ours…*you're* going to…" And the problem was hers. All hers. Since that day, Dave had done very little save criticize and spout behavioral techniques to soothe their crying child.

She resents Dave and his all-too-busy schedule and longs for the day when her own career could take precedence over her personal life. She resents all that time he spends away from Jerri. She resents his pompous air when he does quell the screeching little thing. Her life with the "baby from hell" (Trudy's brother Jim's name for Jerri) is a daily stress. Trudy hasn't seen her brother in over a year, and although that suits Dave just fine, Trudy misses Jim and longs to be in his company. Dave, with his condescending sing-song vocal pattern, would say that Jim is a drinker and not a good influence over a small child. Trudy resents Dave for the distance he has placed between herself and her brother.

She keeps wondering what is to stop her from just walking out. Abandoning both Jerri and Dave; leaving her obtuse husband and the child he wanted. She lies to herself, telling herself she never really wanted to adopt; abandoning them would ensure her freedom. She remembers that when she agreed to this decision, she secretly hoped their marriage would improve. Before they adopted Jerri, Dave was spending all too much time on the web, and Trudy thought the shared responsibility of a child would distract Dave. Maybe it would remove his attention from that mind-stagnating device and focus them instead on his wife and their little girl.

To hear Dave speak to others, theirs is a near perfect marriage, and the girl, although troubled, is a sweet little angel that they are blessed to have. But in reality, the laptop sits upon Dave's lap more than their little girl does. Sometimes Trudy would like to rip it from him and put Jerri in his arms and become "webified" herself. A zombie of sorts who could tune out their teary child. She too could glaze over and lose herself in an electronic world far away from both Dave and Jerri.

Ignorance being bliss, Trudy doesn't want to know exactly where Dave goes on that device. Once she asked him if he was a chat-room visitor. He told her of a brief time before AOL's popularity; when he made the rounds in certain chat rooms but found it all quite dull. Dave claims he uses it to read students' and colleagues' papers on developmental disorders, both behavioral and physiological, in order to one day publish a work that will rock the psychological world. To date he still is working on his opus, and Trudy resents the many hours he is connected to that machine. They are hours he could be giving Trudy as time away from the endless well of tears known as Jerri Lee Lawrence.

III

On a plane, Dr. Dave Lawrence closes his eyes and laptop hoping to find rest. Three days in Cleveland, two nights at home, and then he'll be off again for Dr. Felding's seminar on language acquisition and developmental delays based on birth order. Felding is an ass, but Dave, who suffers from sleep deprivation, looks forward to the trip if only to sleep alone in a king-sized bed. Between Jerri Lee's 1:00 a.m. terror attacks (sometimes lasting two hours) and Trudy's fretful nights, Dave sleeps very little in his own bed. When all is calm, when both girls actually do sleep, Dave lies awake missing those nights when he and Trudy slept without disruption. So, even when he can rest, even when he can catch up on all the sleep he has missed, Dr. Dave lies awake missing what once was and longs to have it back again. His life was settled, was comfortable before the baby came, and now he regrets ever wanting Jerri Lee.

Dave did want this child though. Watching his associates, siblings, and friends wrapped up in the lives of their children had Dave envious of their joy. He pushed Trudy into the decision to adopt. She was content as they were—maybe a bit too content, he thinks now, choosing not to remember her intrusion into his cyber-play. Now, her constant nagging that he is spending too much time plugged into his computer finds him plugged in all the more.

She doesn't know of his other life there. Jakhammer1@aol.com is the confident, sometimes cocky persona Dave adopts while in the chat rooms. Although Trudy is unaware that this side of Dr. Dave exists, Jak is quite popular with the ladies who visit roughtalk.net.

The vibrating thump of the plane's landing rouses Dave from his rest, and although his genitals swell from thinking upon his latest conversation with dirtygirl99, no one would notice. His pleated pants leave plenty of room for this secret thrill. Besides, his thick but quite stubby penis is barely noticeable even when he is naked, much to the dismay of his loving but quite conventional wife, Trudy.

Earlier in their marriage, knowing he could not satisfy her, Dave purchased a marital device and tried to introduce it into their sex play. She wanted none of it. It wasn't that big, he told her. It was thick, like himself, but much longer than his own apparatus. Trudy was put off by the whole idea. Trudy prefers for Dave to satisfy her orally instead of having that lumbering wad of rubber make its way in and out of her. The one time they used the thing, he convinced himself that she was disgusted by his deep fascination with the thing he secretly names Jak.

Every so often he removes Jak from its hiding place and masturbates wildly. He fantasizes that Jak is actually his own member and strokes both himself and the rubber Jak with one essential difference: Jak requires a full palm stroke, whereas little Dave only needs a few good tug-tugs with index finger and thumb to get the job done.

Upon leaving the airport he considers stopping at his office, plugging in to see if 199 is online. A few quick comments, a few dirty words, and maybe he'll be less tense when he arrives home. His release is quick and neat. An old Burger King napkin awaits the deposit, and within minutes Dave is riding home to take part in Jerri's first Asian adoptee support group. He found them online one evening after he and dirtygirl did their thing. He keyed in "asian adopt support" and had come up with seven different groups in their area. He is curious to meet the parents, but mostly he wants to see the children. He wants to see if they share Jerri's propensity for tears.

IV

Trudy is distracted. The play area is alive with the squeals of seven toddlers plus Jerri. There are two Vietnamese, two Korean, one Thai, and two Japanese, Jerri Lee making an even eight. Bert and Sylvia were speaking of the difficulties adopting their Tommy. Phil and Beth were telling Dave how frightened their little Tiffany was at the first meeting (play time) of this arm of A.A.S.S. (Asian Adopt Support Services). Music to influence learning, starting early with letter identification, preschools: all are topics of conversation at the Lawrences' on this first night of support. Trudy hears it all, nodding in agreement, saying, "I see" much too often. But her real attention is upon her daughter. Dave, who is better trained to look interested when bored, is also eying his little girl and is somewhat amazed. They exchange a look of disbelief and understand—as married folk often do—a host of statements that they would share if they were alone and discussing this all-too-rare sight.

For Jerri Lee is mesmerized. Children play about her and Jerri, usually quite possessive of her toys, watches happily as other children like herself play, giggle, and take in this new environment. She gets up from her place on the floor and toddles over to her Playskool family house. Kneeling, Jerri looks inside the tiny bathroom at the patch of reflective paper that simulates a full-length mirror. She stares into her distorted image, and then looks about at these new faces around her. She stands herself up, toddles over to Karlie, and takes Karlie's face in her pudgy fingers. Jerri smiles, looks over to the adults and up at their faces, and then looks back at the children that play about her. Awareness without understanding confuses the three-year-old adoptee. She is happy, but she does not understand why.

Three hours of play for the children come to an end, and as the couples begin to bundle up their little ones, Jerri is in distress. Her face scrunches: Eyebrows meet, lips purse, and soon Jerri is wailing. Beth tries to soothe Jerri, saying, "We'll be back, honey. Tiffany will come back to play." This only makes it worse. She latches onto the tired Tiffany and refuses to let go. The parents have to peel back Jerri's tiny fingers from Tiffany's pink parka. The piercing screeches of Jerri Lee Lawrence can be heard after they shut their Toyota Corolla's doors and are only muted when Phil turns on the engine.

V

Jerri Lee is five. Her parents have invited both their families, Dave's colleagues, and the parents and children from the Asian support group to the celebration. The only time Jerri is agreeable is when she is these children's company, and both Dave and Trudy would like their friends and families to see how wonderful a child their teary and sometimes uncontrollable little girl can be. They have spared no expense. The party, a bit much for a five-year old, is at Brickmills, an old Long Island estate attached to a working farm. The kids will have pony rides and will be entertained by a group of employees whose sole purpose is to keep them amused while the parents amuse themselves with food and drink. A large play area with a miniature house sits behind the veranda. The children will dine there, and when it is time for cake, the guests can gather around a picnic table and sing. The place is ideal for the Lawrences, and Dave is convinced that when his parents see Jerri Lee laughing and playing, they just may rethink their opinion that adopting Jerri Lee was a mistake.

Trudy too is anxious. Her brother, the only member of her family who articulates what the rest of her family thinks and whispers among one another, ought to change his mind when he sees Jerri Lee behaving like a well-adjusted, happy little girl. Well adjusted, Trudy thinks, as long as she is with her play group. Her thoughts and ideas, the ones she keeps to herself, are broadcast, all too audibly, by her brother Jim. She holds onto his arm, looking down on the happy children, and says, "Look, Jim, look how happy Jerri Lee is."

"Yes. She is definitely happy. Happy when she is in the company of others like herself. Other Asians." The silence from those within earshot is uncomfortable. Some guests, unaware of Jerri Lee's regular behavior, look upon Jim as a politically incorrect bigot and shy away from him while coffee, cake, and liqueurs are served.

There are five Barbie dolls as gifts for Jerri Lee—two collector's editions and three sets of themed Barbie: Surfer Barbie, Executive Barbie, and the only one that remains headed: International Barbie. International Barbie is actually called Suzy and although her hair is jet black, the face and body are still that of the actual Barbie. In no way does she resemble an Asian, yet her outfit—a cheap red silk embroidered kimono, decorated with a golden dragon—is held tight in the grasp of the sleeping Jerri Lee Lawrence. The rest are in a gift bag with the exception of Executive Barbie. Her head couldn't be found. It floats face up in the koi pond under a lily leaf. The koi keep nipping at it, seeing it as a new treat. The bodiless head with eyes painted open keeps bobbing beneath the surface, rising again to float around with an ever-pert expression.

The ride home is insufferable. Extricating Jerri Lee from Tiffany left Beth and Phil's little girl with deep scratches on her thin arms. Jerri ought to be better adjusted, Trudy thinks. Dave is always working on different behavioral techniques, but today was the last straw. Finally, when the tired little girl, exhausted from the day, exhausted from a twenty-minute crying jag, falls asleep in her car seat, Trudy says, "Dave, I just can't do this anymore." It is not the first time she's uttered this phrase, and it is most definitely not the last.

VI

Two days after the birthday, Dave prescribes a mild dose of a Prozac derivative to his adopted daughter. At first she resists this tiny pill, but her parents use a little blackmail: "You have to take the pill if you want to play with Suzy…go to the playground…see Tiffany, Melanie or Shannon…have this yummy vanilla ice cream." Jerri Lee becomes accustomed to the morning ritual of pill and then breakfast. Her behaviors improve after two weeks. She no longer runs about intent on disrupting their once quiet home. And the crying, the ceaseless stream of tears and hiccups of distress, is almost nonexistent. However, before she naps and before her mother tucks her in for the night, Jerri Lee always whimpers and releases a few of the ever-familiar tears.

Dave thinks himself a failure for finally giving in to Trudy's demand that something be done. After all his training and conferences with colleagues, Dave could not latch on to a model of behavioral training to quell his little girl's unhappiness. He resents his wife for the ultimatum that he either explore drug therapy or explore the dynamics inherent in being a single parent in charge of an inconsolable five-year-old.

The relief that Trudy feels is replaced by a piteous feeling of doom. This child has never been comfortable with her or with Dave for that matter. As an infant she was restless and irritable. As a toddler she was destructive and teary. Now as a preschool student under the influence of drug therapy Jerri Lee is controllable, agreeable, and more pleasant than ever before. But Trudy feels that just under this skin of Jerri Lee's new found pleasantness lies a sleeping dragon, a dragon that breathes petulance and fiery rebellion. Trudy fears the day this dragon awakens and their lives will once again return to restless nights and exhausting days consoling the inconsolable.

VII

Six months after her drug therapy began, Jerri Lee turns to Trudy and says, "Mom, tell me about my real mother." Trudy has nothing to say. There is nothing to say. She looks down upon the glazed-over black eyes of her little girl, not knowing how to address this. They never met the woman who bore Jerri Lee. The adoption process does not allow this, and although Jerri Lee knew she was a very much-wanted child, nothing was ever said of how she became an adoptee. Internally, Trudy debates whether to tell Jerri Lee that in China couples are expected to limit their families to one child. Heavy taxes on a second or third child and government propaganda encourage the Chinese to limit their nation's ever-increasing population. Besides, there is a negative attitude toward the female gender in China. All this runs through her mind, but Trudy cannot find the words to sate Jerri Lee's curiosity.

Looking down at Jerri Lee, Trudy thinks the easiest way to confront this is to be simple, direct, and honest. . Hearing an account of Dave and Trudy's fantasies prior to the adoption would not satisfy the child. Trudy thinks of the lies her own parents told her as a child and the betrayal she felt upon learning there was no Santa Claus, Easter Bunny, or Tooth Fairy. Trudy wishes Dr. Dave were here to explain to their daughter the why and where-fore of Jerri Lee's being thousands of miles away from her birth mother.

It would be so easy to just lie. Tell the girl that her birth parents died in an earthquake and she and Dave saved the infant from a succession of orphanages and foster homes. How easy it would be to say that her birth mother was a friend of both Trudy's and Dave's and asked them on her deathbed to raise her fatherless infant. It amazes Trudy that all this runs through her mind in a matter of seconds while their little girl waits for an explanation.

"Jerri, I'm your real mommy. I've held you and cared for you since you were an infant. It was the best day of my life when first I held you. Your birth mother never held you—never even saw you. She was very sick and couldn't take care of you. That's why Daddy and I adopted you."

"Where is she now?"

It would be so easy to say she died. Maybe that would end her questions and allow the child some closure, as Dave would say. But all she says is, "I don't know," and tries to console the child by gently stroking Jerri's lustrous straight hair.

"Jerri, sometimes adults do things because they think it is best for everyone. Your real mother..." and in an instant resentment builds. Trudy wants to scream at her daughter. *Yes, my daughter! I fed you, rocked you, kissed your inconsolable brow, and tried everything within my power to nurture and mother you!* "Your real mother...gave us the greatest gift any couple can have.... A baby; a baby of our own." She kneels, looking into Jerri's jet black eyes, hoping the child will bury herself in Trudy's embrace. Tears well in her own eyes, yet she sees nothing in Jerri Lee's expression that seems embraceable. If she needed a word to describe the child's look, indifference would be most apt.

"One day I am going to find my real mommy." Jerri turns, walks over to her dollhouse, and speaks her gibberish talk to her playthings. It is then that Trudy allows her own well of tears to empty onto her flushed cheeks.

VIII

Dave is less and less interested in dirtygirl99. Even Jak has lost its allure. Dave burns with a passion he does not dare admit even to himself. But deep down, Dave knows. Deep, deep under the soul of Dr. Dave Lawrence lies a gentle beast who craves the touch of his adopted little girl. Never has he touched her, or showed her this very ugly side, but her every move—each turn of her head, each look of frustration, even that piteous face she makes when consumed with tears—excites him. So much so that he conjures up her image when he tug-tugs on his somewhat lacking appendage.

He is always away from home when he allows himself this shameful thought and action to satisfy his libido. Intellectually he knows he should seek help—maybe a few sessions with his mentor—but to date, he hasn't admitted this to anyone; he knows he'd be ruined. Besides, he has not allowed and will not allow himself to go over the line. He assures himself of this by distancing himself with work. Attending as many seminars as he can either give or participate in will limit his contact with his little girl. Now that Jerri Lee is almost thirteen and going into the ninth grade, she is all the more appealing. Sending her away to a camp with her other adopted friends for a month will be a great time to possibly reconnect with his wife to keep his secret lust hidden like Jak his rubber alter ego.

Two years ago Trudy started working, and she is seemingly consumed by her menial tasks as librarian at Jerri Lee's former elementary school. She grows further apart from Dave each day. She is home by 4:30, available on days when Jerri needs carting from soccer, volleyball, field hockey, or dance. Some sort of dinner is either defrosted or sent out for. They eat a lot of food prepared by someone else. Dave misses the days when they cooked together, read to each other, or just enjoyed themselves listening to their old LPs.

Dave promises himself that on the very first night Jerri is away at camp, he will bring home lobsters and big steaks for a home-cooked meal like before and try to recapture what he thinks once was. That girl of theirs robs them of their selfish pursuits. Dave thinks of his dark, hidden side and hopes that four weeks for Jerri at Camp Lotus will help him put aside these nasty thoughts and return to his former self. Yet his hopes diminish when his mind's eye wanders back to his budding little girl, and he tug-tugs himself for one last guilty pleasure.

IX

On the ride up the New York State Thruway, Jerri, sprawled across the back seat of their Aerostar minivan, watches but does not listen to the DVD, *House of Horrors*. She has seen the film too many times to count, but letting it play on while her ears are plugged into her iPod has got to irk her parents. The screams alone make Trudy's neck tighten as the girl runs from the masked, knife wielding sociopath. Twice Dave has asked her to lower the volume. Twice she has complied, but she slowly works the volume up one notch at a time until she's asked again.

The green trees blur against the wide windows of the van as they near Camp Lotus, and Jerri Lee wonders if Tiffany and Melanie will be there when she arrives. The Lawrences offered to drive both girls up with them, but both sets of parents preferred to drive their respective daughters themselves. This was a new experience for their adopted treasures, and they wanted to be as much a part of it as they could.

Sometimes Jerri fantasizes that her real parents, her unknown nameless Chinese parents, will come and find her. Take her back to China where she'll feel at home. The house she's known all her life has never, not once as long as she can remember, felt like home. Her real parents will one day ring the Lawrences' doorbell and demand that they relinquish their adoptive rights and take Jerri Lee home.

She is angry: angry with her birth parents, angry with her adopted parents, and according to her counselor, angry at the world, which isn't any way to live. Yet the girl just cannot help herself. She baits her mother into petty arguments, but her father, that pudgy mountain of a man, is harder to engage. He acquiesces to her whims, sometimes siding with Jerri in their mother-daughter disagreements. This sends Trudy into days of numbing silence.

In her sweetest voice she asks one question. It is really the only conversation between parents and child on the three-hour ride upstate. "Whatever made you name me Jerri Lee?" And their answer only serves to push their wanted child further away from Dave and Trudy Lawrence.

X

Jerri Lee knew the answer and had known the answer for a very long time. She remembers how Trudy and Dr. Dave used to dance in the living room to that noise they call music. Remembers them both moving the coffee table against the wall, remembers them tossing off their shoes to have what they called a sock hop. Remembers how she secretly wanted to hop with them, but something always stopped her from joining in. Dr. Dave, her make-pretend father, would pick her up and swing her like a rag doll. Jerri was quick to put an end to that by screaming and poking her index fingers into her ears. Eventually the dancing stopped, and so did the music.

Crying, screaming, and being sullen would not only get Jerri her way but would render the added bonus of keeping that woman, her make-pretend mother, at a safe distance. Dr. Dave had her hearing tested regularly because of the distress he'd see on her face when she heard, "You shake my nerves and rattle my brains. Too much love drives a man insane. You broke my will, but what a thrill: Goodness gracious, great balls of fire!" Her hearing was fine; it was what she was hearing that was the problem. Over time their music had morphed from assorted oldies into light classical from the radio, and Jerri Lee couldn't be happier.

XI

"They named me after a creep who sang songs about his enflamed nuts! A guy who married his thirteen-year old cousin! Nice, huh? That's it. I'm changing my name."

Jerri and her campmates are sitting around their hut during a free hour at Camp Lotus. The cots are all bedded with green quilts with the camp's symbol, a white lotus flower, embroidered at the center.

"C'mon Jerri, I like your name. It's much nicer than Tiffany. Tiffany sounds like I should be blonde and vacant between my ears."

"At least the Lee sounds Chinese. Melanie...I'm named after a folk singer who sang about her roller skates without her own key. What the hell was the key for?"

"That's it! Henceforth, call me...L-I, Li."

"Christ, Jerri—er, I mean Li—who uses words like 'henceforth'? You're so angry! I like you Jer—Li, but...you're always finding ways to hurt your parents."

Li puts up her hand and closes her eyes; it works with Trudy and Dave but doesn't work on Melanie. "The Lawrences are not my parents!"

"Yes. They are your parents, Jerri Lee Lawrence. They care for you, educate you, feed you. You should be grateful.... In China you'd have nothing!"

"Yes I would! I would have my mother!" Li cries. Unlike the tears she can turn on and off with her parents, these stream forth and sting as they trickle down her cheeks. She leaves the group and heads into the woods and away from the common house, past the boys' camp and up the slope to the watchtower long ago abandoned by the county. The boys sneak off there to smoke cigarettes, and as she begins her ascent, she hears the rustling of feet on the platform. Two boys with guilty expressions stare at her as she emerges from the cutout in the floor.

The twins, Max and Sam Anderson, were almost fifteen, and wherever one was, the other was always nearby and ready for fun. Jerri has known them since her playgroup began and has always been envious of them for having one another. She likes them. Here was a situation that would make her home life much easier. If she had a sibling who looked exactly like she did, and then maybe she wouldn't feel so alone.

"What are you doing?" Sam always wore red and Max blue; it was how everyone could tell them apart. Their parents used to dress them that way so they would know which boy was which. So, along with the white Camp Lotus T-shirt, each boy wore shorts of the identifying hue.

"Nothing. I'll leave if you were doing some secret twin shit. But if you wouldn't mind, I'd like to hide out here." As Jerri Lee stares from one face to the other, she thinks something is wrong. She could always tell them apart even without their color coding, and something is amiss. Max has thicker eyebrows and furrows his brow when lost in thought, yet he is wearing red shorts. At that moment of cognition she asks, "Hey—what gives? Sam, why are you wearing Max's shorts? Playing a little mind fuck on someone?"

Both boys try to defend their lie, telling Jerri she is nuts, but Jerri will have none of it. She scrutinizes them both and silences their pathetic pretense with, "Max, Sam—I've known you both all my life. You can't bullshit me." She pierces their deception with her incredulous stare, and they both plead for her to keep their secret.

"And we just wanted…"

Max interrupts, "…wanted to see if Mr. Keough would notice."

"Tell the truth, Sam. Keough always brags that he can. He's been doing that since we were kids, and I told Sam he couldn't, and I was right!"

"No you weren't…I think he knew and just didn't let on."

"Noooo…way!"

"Way! You weren't there. He always talks to you like you're the smarter one—almost an equal. He talks about books and education shit to you. He thinks you're going to be a great teacher. Me—sports. Stats and who do I think will win the series. He offered to lend me—I mean you—his most prized possession, *The Complete Works of Dylan Thomas.* Come on! If it were me, for real, I'd get *Amazing: The Story of the 1969 Mets.*"

Jerri is in awe. Just the thought of being someone else for a few hours appeals very much to her. The boys prattle on with their stupid argument. Jerri thinks on their escapade and blurts out, "Dylan Thomas, the Welsh poet. He offered you Dylan Thomas?"

"Not me, but me as Max."

"Dylan fucking Thomas! Are you interested in depressing poetry?

Max stares at her, adding a quick, "No…but last year—remember, Sam?—right after Nanny Hughes died, he read that poem. I cried. But not from the poem he was reading. I watched Mom while he spoke. Her whole body shook like she was cold. I don't know…now he thinks I'm the sensitive one who likes to talk about feelings. He's kind of creepy."

"Do you do this with your parents?" Jerri assumes that they will lie and is ready to pounce on them if they even attempt it.

The boys look at each other as if for permission. Both stare at Jerri and glance sideways before they utter in unison, "Yes."

"That's great! Your secret is safe with me." She sits with her back against the rough wood planks and lets out a long breath of air. This is the best she has felt in weeks, and she savors this bond with the Anderson twins. "Tell me about it."

"About what?" they both say.

"About your parents. When did you first do it? Were you scared they would catch you? Do you do it at your school? Tell me everything…. I'm dying to know."

It didn't take long for the boys to open up, and Jerri was enthralled with each tale. Her favorite was when Max pretended to be Sam during the state literacy tests. Sam pretended to be sick that day and was able to convince his parents that a) he was Max and b) he was sick. And on the day of the retest, they were able to do the same thing again in reverse. So Sam took the test twice. Surprisingly to both their language arts teacher and their parents, Sam, it seems, is actually the better student. Now they all cannot understand why Sam doesn't score higher during his regular classes and has yet to make the honor roll. Dr. Dave, Jerri's dad, told the Andersons that sometimes that is just the way it is with geniuses. When Jerri heard that she nearly keeled over from laughter at her adopted father's assessment.

"He's an ass."

"You're telling me! I had to sit in his office for six fucking weeks while he played motivational speaker. I would have gone eight if it weren't for my brother here…. He took my place twice."

Max smiles at his brother, nodding in agreement. Both Jerri and his brother Sam were correct: Dr. Dave is an ass. "Hey Jerri, you're not going to tell, are you?"

"Never." This is the first of many secrets that Jerri will share with the boys. "I hate them. I hate them both." She begins to choke back tears she can't understand and adds, "I think I hate her more than him."

"You don't really hate them, Jerri. They're your parents—you shouldn't hate them." Max looks to Sam for support. "This is just a phase all girls go through at one time or another." Now Max does his impression of Dr. Dave's condescending rhythmic speech pattern, "Eventually…at one point…in their development…all daughters hate their mothers."

Jerri screams, "She *is* not my mother and don't call me that anymore!" The boys look down upon her and see Jerri clench her fists, pounding one against the rough planks. "They are both so embarrassing. She is never home anymore, and he never was. He is always off somewhere and I like it that way. At least I don't have to look at him. And she—well, she is *not* my mother. My mother is somewhere in China, and one day I'm going to find her."

"Jerri, don't be stupid. They—"

She cuts him off with, "Do not call me that! My name is Li. Li Fong." She stole the last name from the boy who delivers the Thai food once a week at the Lawrence's.

"Li Fong?" Again they speak as one and Max adds, "Where'd you come up with that?"

"It's my new name. I'm changing it legally as soon as I can! I hate the name the Lawrences gave me. They named me after a perv!"

"A—what?" Again in unison, and Li regurgitates what she learned about the aged rocker from the Internet and as Li puts it, "How stupid can two people be? Naming a Chinese baby after a man who married his thirteen year-old cousin! I hate that name and the Lawrences know I hate it. I made sure of that right before they left me at Camp Low-to-Us!"

The boys are perplexed and are quite intrigued by her anger. It stirs something in Max; something that makes him want to comfort this new girl called Li. Prior to this exchange Max and Sam had seen Li—Jerri back then—only when group got together. They didn't play with this girl aside from the parent interaction portion of the afternoons or evening when group met. Duck, Duck, Goose, the preferred game of the Anderson boys, made Jerri laugh. It wasn't often that Jerri laughed; Max remembers her crying and throwing tantrums most of the time. These past two years, they hadn't seen much of the Lawrences, though. Their group still meets, but it is the parents who gather and not the kids. The kids, now preteens or teenagers, have their own friends, see each other occasionally, and are all together only at Camp Lotus.

Sam is excited by Li. Her power, determination, and defiance turn him on. "Low-to-Us. That's great. Ha! You hate this place?" He looks down on her raven black hair and has the urge to rest his hand on her head and stroke her hair. Li looks up at Sam and smiles at her own joke and repeats his question.

"I asked you first."

"I don't care. Do the Anderson twins hate this place?"

"No." says Max.

"We've outgrown it. Besides, I hate that Mr. Keough. Remember how we were gonna accuse…" Sam is punched by his brother and stops speaking.

"Li, my brother doesn't know when to shut up. We thought about doing something terrible once, but it was just a thought. An ugly thought. Forget he ever brought it up."

"The one thing I can't do is forget. But I can keep it to myself."

They agree to meet again at the watchtower the following day, and for the first time in the short existence of the former Jerri Lee—forevermore Li—she feels less alone.

XII

Camp Lotus prides itself as being a model for idyllic retreat rather than a camp of a more traditional nature. They do have canoeing, volleyball, cookouts, and hiking trips, but here at Camp Lotus they also have yoga and Asian studies, meditation time, and time to indulge the impressionable minds of Asians raised by Americans. Too many times Li had seen or been told that in Asia, the land of her birth, she would have had no rights and possibly no life. The message is there and it is subtle. America is better. Li is angry. Angry with her parents and angry with the world.

During meditation time Li makes her way to the watchtower. Alone she climbs the rickety rungs and sits waiting for the boys. She has brought two cigarettes, stolen from Ms. Dawson's backpack, and hopes the boys have matches. Li is going to smoke. Li is going to cut her hair. Li is going to wear makeup and become anything but a grateful child. She hears them come and makes a wish to the universe: Help me boys. Help me with my plan.

XIII

The last two weeks at Camp Lotus are spent preparing for the annual talent show. Tiffany will play a Mozart piece for flute, accompanied by Mary Alice Keough on piano, Daisuke, the only camper with an actual Asian name, will show a film that he and Troy have worked on since camp began. And others will demonstrate movement and song. There are no contests at Camp Lotus; here every camper is a winner with endless possibilities.

Li has come up with an idea, and Max and Sam love it. They crack up each time they rehearse their fake show. Max will pluck a pipa, a Chinese guitar. Sam, who is supposed to stretch in and out of yoga positions, keeps laughing while Li begins to recite six haiku full of nature imagery. It is full of peace and serenity, and it is all supposed to be serious. Ms. Dawson is not laughing, nor does she understand why Sam is. But his two cohorts do, and when they are at the watchtower, Li rips into Sam and begs his brother Max to beat him up if he blows their surprise.

"It's not going to work if you lose control. You have to stay focused!" Yet the odd thing is, when they rehearse their real act, the one for the last day of camp, the one the parents will see, Sam does it letter perfect.

"I will. I promise. I just think we ought to practice with the water."

And they do. They practice until none of them crack up. They are perfectly straight-faced and are excited by their prank.

"Do you think they'll be embarrassed?" Sam asks.

"Do you think they'll try to stop us?" Max adds.

"Yes and no. I think the parents will be surprised, the counselors will be too stunned to do anything, and I think Ms. Dawson, who might be on to us, may like the idea of the unexpected. What does she always say about the joy of 'live theater'?"

"'You never know what magic will happen when you lose yourself in a performance.'"

It is amazingly done in unison, and what is more fascinating to Li is that both boys are dead on with the distinctive nasal quality of Ms. Dawson's speech.

"I want them to be embarrassed. I want Dr. Dave and Trudy to turn red. I doubt they could feel half of my shame every time I think of that book. I know they still have one, and when I find it, I'm going to burn it like I burned the others."

The boys know the book. Their parents probably still have a copy. Dr. Dave had Valentine's books printed and sent one to all their friends in group. From Dave and Trudy's perspective it was cute: a Valentine from their soon to be potty-trained little doll to her parents and the rest of her world. It contained baby pictures of Mom changing Jerri's diapers, solo pictures of the potty, Jerri sitting on the damn thing looking stressed and the final most embarrassing shot: Dr. Dave holding the pot as little Jerri points to her own turd with a caption that reads: "Jerri Lee and her little Poo!"

Sam makes a promise to himself that when he gets back home; he will find the Anderson's copy of "A Valentine from the Lawrences" and burn it. He hopes that when he tells this to Li, she will see him as more than just a friend.

XIV

They spend the last morning at camp together by the lake. The three of them swim out to the floating dock and lie there anticipating their parents' arrival. They are eager for this afternoon's performance but have stopped talking about it. Instead their talk is of a more serious tone. Bittersweet with the separation of lifelong friends, Li makes both boys promise that they will stay in contact after camp. "Don't blow off the monthly group get-together. I like you both and want us to stay friends."

They forgo lunch and spend the hour before the parents' arrival sharing a stolen cigarette.

"Remember, Sam—do not flinch. And when you do move, exaggerate each thrust. Make it big!"

"I know, Li. Don't worry. I'll make you proud." Sam and Max hope that their performance will forever seal their place in Li Fong's heart. As for their parents, John and Mary Anderson, both brothers doubt either will be proud or very pleased.

XV

The large meditation room doubles as a theater. Meditation classes have been held out on the lawn this last week in order to rehearse and ready the room for Camp Lotus's shining moment. Ms. Dawson has Julie Weitzenbaum lead the yoga hour while she organizes each rehearsal. And what talent there is! Each musical moment is an inspiration: A testament to the dedication of each parent's push to have well-rounded and interesting children. The few dance numbers have real spirit, according to Ms. Dawson. And the poetry portion is near transcendental, a perfect reflection of Camp Lotus's dedication to Asian culture.

After Tim Hathaway's fifty-two-second rendition of the Minute Waltz, the audience erupts with wild applause, and Li is numb. Their rehearsals didn't prepare her for stage fright. The boys, dressed in white pants and T-shirts, are blatantly color coded by their red and blue sweatbands. They take their place and await her arrival. Sam stands stock-still stage left while his brother takes his place on a short stool stage right. Li is dressed as a geisha. In a red silk robe, a white obi, and a wig made from human hair be-decked with strands of fake pearls, she takes center stage. Across her neck is a pole with two buckets attached at each end. Placing the buckets down, she whips out a fan, whisking it open with all the deftness of an actual geisha. She titters seductively, concealing her ruby painted lips behind a half moon of filigreed ivory. She bows to her two cohorts and begins an elaborate fan dance. It is one she copied from a movie she has seen too many times. *The King and I* was a tape the Lawrences owned, along with *The Sound of Music, The Wizard of Oz, Singin' in the Rain,* and other musicals, but it was *The King and I* that Li would watch again and again as a child. The children looked like Li, and she liked that. The fan seems to float in the air from Li's delicate touch. Offstage, Ms. Dawson beams at this sullen camper performing with such grace and poise.

A loud pluck from the pipa and Li begins to speak sweetly, shyly, yet with a loudness that can be heard in the back row.

"You shake-a my nerves. You rattle-a my brains…"

Mimicking a caricature Asian with little command of the English lan-guage, she continues as Sam contorts himself into the crane. Standing on one leg, Sam is eager for Li's cue. Another tinny pluck and Sam looks to his brother without expression.

Sam stretches both legs placing his hands on his cheeks and looks as if he were screwing his face off with slow rotations of his neck. Three sharp plucks from the pipa, and Max places his instrument on the floor.

"Too much-a ruve drive a man insane. You broke-a-my will...oooo what a thrill..."

Sam stops rotating his neck. Keeping his hands firmly attached to the sides of his face he begins to rock his hips from side to side.

"Good-a-ness, gracious..." she lowers her fan and on cue Max leans over toward the bucket closest to him. While in a bent position, he lifts it and waits. Sam, thrusting his hips keeps his hands firmly attached to his contorted expression.

"Great balls on fire!"

With one swift movement Max tosses the entire bucket of water at his brother's gyrating crotch. The campers laugh. Sam's pants, wet and now translucent, reveal that he is wearing his brother's ruby red Speedo. His hands rush from his face and down to his crotch in an exaggerated movement of surprise. The three begin to hop from one foot to the other and make a complete circle. When they arrive at their original positions, Max picks up the pipa, striking three shrill notes. His brother begins to manipulate his body into the cobra while Li lets out a high-pitched guttural sound reminiscent of a loon yodeling for its mate.

"Kiss-a me Baby..."

Sam puckers up and Li titters before covering her mouth with the fan.

"...woo feels good. Hold me baby, well...I want to ruve you rike a ruver should!"

Sam manipulates his body into the downward dog, raising his buttocks with deliberate up and down motions.

"You fine..."

He stops humping the air and another loud pluck has him jump to his feet with his legs firmly pushed together.

"...so kind..."

Sam begins to shake like he is about to erupt as Li continues,

"I wanna tell the world that you're mine, mine, mine."

The three begin to hop about in place. Max tosses the pipa into the air, catches it, and plucks. *Thwoing! Thwoing! Thwoing!*

Ms. Dawson is slack-jawed. Her mouth is agape and she is keenly aware of her dry throat. She knows she should stop this but is so very caught by surprise that she does nothing. She watches the geisha and the boy hop about, and does nothing. She watches Sam Anderson (or is it Max?) toss the pipa and does nothing. The geisha flirts from behind her fan to both boys and makes that awful noise again, and it makes Ms. Dawson think of a swan choking.

With the fan at her chin, Li contorts her face with tension, "I chew my nails…"—big sigh—"I twiddle my…'scuse me Joe…what twiddle?"

She bows left; she bows right, and shrugs her shoulders while both boys twiddle their thumbs and continues, "Hee hee. Twiddle thumbs."

Thwoing! Ta da Twoing!

Sam throws himself onto the floor and begins to enter the crab position. The up-and-down motions of his crotch, slow and deliberate, have Ms. Dawson, Mr. Keough, and quite a few parents uncomfortable. The campers are laughing: They all get the joke, and the boys are really stealing much of Li's thunder.

"I'm rearleee nervous, it sure is fun! Come on baby, drive me crazy. Good-a-ness gracious…" Li begins to fan Sam the humping crab with broad suggestive strokes. Li fans the damp crotch of Sam while making expressions of excitement and revulsion in broad pantomime. John Anderson rises from his seat, and then sits, wondering why this insulting thing was allowed in the show. Someone should have stopped this before it even started. Why is Max (or is that Sam?) allowing himself to be used in such a way, thrusting his hips like that…to, of all things, that horrible girl's recitation of "Great Balls of Fire"? This is causing his stomach to burn and his neck to chafe from sweat and starch. Dr. Dave's girl—it just has to be her, he thinks.

This time when Jerri Lee says, "Great balls of fire!" she is fanning Sam's crotch. She bows at her waist so her face is just atop the up and down motions of that Anderson boy. Dr. Dave is uncomfortable for a host of reasons. But the one that will never be mentioned is the uncomfortable yet pleasant stirring in his tiny member.

Max plucks one long *thwoing,* places the pipa on his stool, and grabs the second bucket. Li doesn't move but stares wide-eyed as if in a trance. Sam raises his reddened crotch closer and closer to her painted red mouth. Max tosses the water just as planned into the stare of the former Jerri Lee Lawrence, newly baptizing her Li Fong.

The campers laugh. The parents do not. Li stands, Sam jumps up with the help of his brother Max, and the two boys smile their widest as Li clasps their hands. They bow as one unit. They come up and the boys take one step back, applauding their friend's performance.

"I dedicate this to my parents, Dr. Dave and Trudy Lawrence. Thank you." She bows and exits. The boys remove the pipa and stool, remembering to pull down the screen for the final portion of the show, the film by Daisuke.

Stage lights are abruptly shut off. Early morning mountain mist begins to emerge on the screen, giving John, Mary, Trudy, and Dr. Dave time to plan a course of action. Li discards her wig and robe backstage. She bolts out the back door and heads for the watchtower for one last chance to be together with her partners before they have to face their parents, Ms. Dawson, and possibly the pasty James Keough. Somewhere down deep in her psyche she thinks: *Goodness, gracious…what have I done?*

XVI

Things were never the same after camp. Their ride home is silent. Silence was never uncomfortable for Li, and she is not in the least bit uncomfortable. Her parents, however, are pink-eared with shame and mighty uncomfortable. The only conversation to occur after the talent show was Trudy Lawrence's low and rather sad observation that Jerri must really hate them both. Li thinks that she doesn't hate them at all. She remembers Max posing a similar sentiment, "You must really hate the Lawrences." But Li doesn't hate them. After all, she remembers what Tiffany, Sam and Max said: they are the only parents she has ever known. As other cars speed by down the thruway, Li thinks of many things to say, but like Ms. Dawson, says and does nothing.

Dr. Dave attempts to console his wife with a long-winded explanation of teenage rebellion and how lashing out at those closest to the teen is an act of independence. Trudy should not take things personally, as this phase of Jerri's development is quite normal. He begins to add things he's garnered from Dr. Ann Silvano's recent paper on teenage angst, and both women let him drone on, lost in their own angst and discomfort.

Li wants to say something, anything to end the tedium of Dr. Dave. Instead, she allows the ride to soothe her and falls deep into one of her reunion fantasies. A reunion with her birth mother is something she has thought about for a long, long time. It gives her pleasure, but this time her mother is not a career woman or the wife of an ambassador who had a liaison with a diplomat. No. This time she lets her mind wander through narrow streets with doorways open to exquisite garden courtyards. It is there she sees this new mother, the one that the government forced into giving up her only daughter. She is dressed in simple garb, a silk lime green quilted jacket festooned with braided black buttons. Her hair is pulled back, and her smile, bright and large, waits to embrace her daughter. They embrace and tears well up in the eyes of her fantasy mother and in her own eyes as well. Li's new mother suffers daily since they took her newborn girl away. She beckons her daughter to sit beside her, and Li opens her eyes to see the back of the Lawrences' heads and their driveway.

XVII

Max and Sam were true to their word and arrived at the McClarin's annual Labor Day gathering. Erin McClarin, a year younger than Li, would be
entering ninth grade with Li. Bumped up from her eighth-grade class; Erin
was filled with enthusiasm and dread. Her parents, Bob and Nancy, beam as
they announce the success of their little girl. Max signals to Li to meet out
front. He hands her his package wrapped in a blue handkerchief. Li hugs her
friend, thanking him for the return of her shame, and Max beams. It doesn't
take long before Sam and Erin catch up with his brother and Li. Erin, seeing
the Valentine in Li's hand, is curious as to why she'd be carting that awful
book around.

"I'm going to burn it, like I did the others." Erin tells them to wait and
dashes into her home, returning with the McClain's copy. Li thinks that her
"brainiac" fellow ninth-grader is not as bad as she once perceived. Erin was
not at camp this summer, preferring instead the accelerated math program
at her school, and only heard about their performance from Melissa and
Tiffany.

The boys had much explaining to do to both their parents and told
them that the idea for the show was not all Li's. They bore much of the responsibility of their performance. Computer privileges were cut off for two
weeks, and both boys did an excellent job of atoning and winning back the
favor of both John and Mary Anderson. They explained that Li was reluctant about the plan, and Max had convinced her that everyone would laugh
and think it was all good fun. How wrong he was. After one week of disappointed looks, with a coolness he had not known before, Max apologized
promising never to shame his parents again. Sam did pretty much the same
but, being a little more rebellious than his brother, added that if he had to
do it all over again, he would.

He said Li was a sorrowful girl who all during their time at camp was
miserable. But during their rehearsals, she came out of her shell with his
brother and himself and was less unhappy. The logic and sensitivity touched
Mary. She tousled his hair saying that what they did was wrong, "even if it
was for the right reason."

Since their performance, Trudy has stopped trying to win her daughter's affection and has left Li alone. It was the desired outcome, and Li finds that being alone is what she has always known. She felt it as a baby, and she feels it still today, but here with Max, Erin and Sam, Li is less alone. As she watches yet another copy of the Valentine her parents so lovingly created burn, Li allows part of her rage to burn away with it and decides her transformation does not have to be so obvious. Slow and deliberate. With a controlled determination, she vows she'll make it through this and one day return to China and find her birth mother.

XVIII

True to her promise, Li transforms herself from rebellious youth to young adult during her first two years of high school. She keeps her hair short, but gone are the black fingernails and severe make up. Gone is the leather as well, with the exception of a thin black dog collar. She wears this with a Chinese coin attached by brass wire to the ring at the buckle, and no matter what her outfit, she wears this daily.

Li excels in math and science and has partnered with Erin in study groups and class projects. Her parents are pleased with their daughter's newfound respect for herself. So pleased, in fact, that they allow her to redecorate her room and equip it with a new entertainment center, TV, DVD, Apple notebook, and cell phone and a stereo that could blow out her bedroom windows. Yet not once, since the walls were painted scarlet red and the ceiling metallic gold, has either Lawrence ever had to ask Li to turn down the volume.

Junior year finds the girls secretary and treasurer of their class, captain and co-captain of the field hockey team, and recipients of the Neal Peabody Math and Science award. This last achievement means so very much to Erin and the McClarins that a celebration was held in their honor at Erin's home. Sam and Max were there, as were Tiffany and Melanie, but it was the Anderson boys both girls long to see. After an hour or so of accepting the congratulations of friends and family, (extended family, as Li is always quick to remind everyone), the four friends unite in the upstairs playroom, now a storage area, at the McClarin's home. Both Max and Sam are surprised by the girl's determination.

"…only natural for you to be…"

Li cuts her friend and partner off with, "Don't be so prudish! You both know you would have done it at camp if I was willing. Christ! Max, what is wrong with you two? You've always been up for a little fun, what's happened to you?"

"Sam," says Erin, using her sweetest voice, "…don't you think by losing our virginity to each other, we'll be able to escape from all that sexual bullshit that plagues relationships. At least we'll know what to expect. We'll know what to do when and if we ever date an outsider."

"Outsider?" both boys say, and Max adds, "Erin, your reasoning is a little off. Losing your virginity should not be a calculated event."

Now it is the girls' opportunity to speak as one. "Why not?"

Sam chimes in with, "Yeah, why not? You know, bro, we'd be giving up our virgin status as well. I don't think it's a bad idea."

And it wasn't a bad idea after all.

The details of this encounter and the subsequent encounters saw the four of them blossom into adulthood with uncommon ease. Their education and knowledge afforded the four of them safe sexual experimentation. All four had at one time perused Dr. Dave's well-worn copy of *The Joy of Sex* and benefited from its line drawings and easy-to-read directions.

The boys were ever ready and open to most of their play, and after their liaisons were over, Max and Sam went back to their homes content, calm and sleepy. Their parents never knew, but when the girls ended their physical relationship with them, Mary Anderson suspected something when both boys grew at first sad, and then sullen, and a little bit on edge.

Li and Erin were gentle with the Anderson twins and explained their separation with much of the same argument used to begin it. It was the mature thing to do. Soon they all would be off to college, meeting other people, doing other things. Why mess up a perfectly good relationship with love stuff? They would always remember their first gentle and loving partners with respect and care, and who knew what might happen in the course of the next six years?

The girls left for college and although Li, much improved by her slow and determined approach at being civil with her adopted parents, tried to muster up some melancholy at leaving the only home she ever knew, she couldn't conceal her joy. Jim, Trudy's brother, could not stop himself from pointing out the obvious. "She's finally happy. Happy to leave, and don't be too surprised if she never comes home."

But Trudy was sad. After seventeen years of watching her fretful child grow into a woman, she wonders where she went wrong to have no real connection with Li. Although these last few years have been mostly un-eventful, they were also void of any bond.

Dr. Dave was sad as well. His reasons were of a more secretive nature. Gratifying himself with photos of young Asian women could never take the place of his true desire. While in San Francisco last year, he visited a brothel specializing in the art of Asian love-making. He paid extra to have a pretty, young girl and has felt guilty ever since for calling her Jerri Lee all through their session.

Li immerses herself in her life outside the Lawrences' and does not come home. She secures a job and earns enough for living expenses, setting a small amount in a savings account earmarked for her trip home to China. She works overtime and takes on a second job and sometimes holiday work. Within two years Li is completely self-supporting.

Her Asian studies professor is Caucasian. He is about fifty years old, is married with one child, and suffers from a midlife crisis. Professor Manheim teaches Li and his classes with enthusiasm and authority. As one of her fellow classmates puts it, Manheim knows his shit.

And he does know much about Asian customs and politics. Manheim knows as much as any outsider could possibly know about a culture steeped in mystery and intrigue. He even admits that no matter how deep he may delve into the culture; he will always be an outsider. Li thinks that that is true of everyone.

Roger Manheim is also quite versed in the sexual practices presented in the Kama Sutra. That he saves to teach his most eager and motivated students. Usually these classes, held in private tutorial sessions at a studio apartment he keeps on the Lower East Side, are his most enlightening. The excitement he feels seeing these inexperienced girls mature into sexual beings under his tutelage sets his nerves to tingle and his balls to jingle.

Li is an excellent student in both public and private tutorials. During her last year of college, she is Manheim's star student, assistant to the good professor, and the most recent in a long line of overachievers that he beds. Not only does he bed them, but he also teaches them the nuances of Asian lovemaking. But this girl is different from his previous conquests. She is open and ready to learn, but to be quite frank; Li has a sexual hunger that seems insatiable. Roger is so smitten with this girl that to deny her anything is to deny him the pleasure of seeing her delight. Li moves into his studio and makes it her rent-free home.

Within a month, Roger is ready to leave his wife and daughter for Li, but she forbids him to do it. He gives her money whenever she asks and has secured for her a position in his department. This affords her greater freedom and keeps her return-to-China fund increasing at a comfortable and steady rate. He sleeps with her as often as he can, while his desire to be with her grows obsessive. Li is always ready to please the good professor and is grateful to have Roger, but love him she does not.

XIX

Trudy can't remember the last time she'd seen Jerri Lee. It seems to her clouded memory that all those years were someone else's life, someone else's bad dream. At first she kept her relief to herself, sharing it only with her brother Jim. She still refers to Li as Jerri but finds that she thinks less and less of the girl with each passing day. She and Dave stuck it out that first year of college, thinking the girl would want to come home for a holiday, but she didn't. Didn't call, didn't come home, and very much, it seems to Trudy, didn't want anything to do with the two who cared for and reared Jerri Lee Lawrence.

The divorce was agreeable, without animosity. Dave bought her out of the house, and with her settlement she begins a new life, living with her brother Jim. Trudy and Jim rarely speak of the girl who drained so much life out of her. Instead, they focus on this day and every subsequent day with enthusiasm and an eagerness to make up for lost time. They begin competing at ballroom dancing, and over a few years they become immersed in a life as partners on the dance floor and partners in life. Neither sibling has the desire to share their lives with outsiders who could possibly distract them from reaching their goal of a National Championship win. Most people assume they are married, and as far as brother and sister are concerned, it only adds to their allure on the dance floor.

XX

Dr. Dave finally publishes a paper. Although it was not in the area of his specific expertise, it was well received, and he becomes something of an expert on sexual obsessions and the behaviors that lead to fixation. He culled his information from folks he met across the country at various Sex Addicts Anonymous meetings. After two years of amassing the histories of over 1,200 subjects, Dr. Dave Lawrence is able to put together a paper that later becomes a national bestseller. It lands him on speaking circuits, and talk shows have him on as a guest authority whenever they do a show titled something like "Controlling and Conquering Sexual Demons."

He and his editor, Jenny, a petite girl of Korean descent, become friends, and then lovers, soon after the book is published. She likes Dave, but more to the point she likes Dave's alter ego, Jak, and he, without the recriminations of a wife like Trudy, uses Jak to take Jenny to places she had only experienced when alone. His obsession with Asian women and rubber devices flourishes with Jenny, and after a year he marries his editor, inviting both Trudy and Li to their wedding. Neither woman attends the wedding, nor do they send a gift.

XXI

It "creeped" Li "out," as she put it to herself, that her adopted father married an Asian. She sees their picture in the Times. Dr. Dave towers over this diminutive lady as he crouches down, leans forward, and smiles for the camera. She remembers how he'd look at her those last two years of high school. She knows now what she suspected soon after she and the Anderson twin became sexually active: Dr. Dave was hot for his little adopted girl. She'd catch his eyes skimming over her body and think that he knew what she and Sam were doing. And probably he'd like to do the same, and that could help reunite Li with her birth mother.

She sends a belated Best Wishes on Your Nuptials card. She signs it but does not read the sentiment to her adoptive father. Instead she adds a note that she would like to see him, one day soon. Li adds her address and phone number, knowing that he will call. He will call and do what she asks. Roger may not like it, but she was tiring of the good professor anyway. He serves his purpose, but he is here far too often. Mrs. Manheim has been traveling with her aged mother, so Roger has been at the apartment almost every day since they went away. In her head, all the way to the post office, mantra-like, Li repeats and repeats: He will call. He will come. He will do as I say.

XXII

What strikes Dave as completely odd is not that his adopted daughter sent a card at all. Truth be told, when they received the "not attending wedding" card, he just thought he would never again hear from the child he reared. So it is odd to be holding a card from her, but not completely odd. Nor is it that Li uses "Father," which she's been using since her preteen years, instead of "Dave," to address the only father the girl ever knew. Both were odd, yes, but what is completely odd to Dave is that she signed the note Jerri. Something about her neat cursive and seeing the name he and Trudy gave her a lifetime ago, a name she detests, affects him, and he calls her immediately only to get her voice-mail.

"Jerri Lee, this is Dad. Call me." He recites his number.

In his mind, deep down somewhere, is a beautiful, ugly thought, a fantasy that he has engaged in since his daughter began her life outside the Lawrences' He hadn't thought about it for some time now, but after he leaves that message it comes flooding over him like a tide. Slow at first… deliberate in its progression until Dr. Dave, world expert on sexual fixation, is engulfed in his own obsession, one that is only quelled by the new Mrs. Dr. Dave but not eradicated.

Jerri always asks for forgiveness. This is how the fantasy begins. She asks Dave to forgive her for being so selfish and unappreciative. She asks that he love her like a good father. "Protect me, father…. I am so very sorry for disrespecting you. Please forgive me." And each and every time, he forgives Jerri. Enfolding her in his thick arms, he hugs her and pats her head. It is a nice thought, reconciling with his daughter, and it pleases Dr. Dave greatly. Yet there was a time when it would go further, and his pleasure would come after he removes her robe, caressing her tiny breasts. Sometimes he delays his forgiveness in this horrendous fantasy until after she does things to him…and for him. Each and every time in this forgiveness fantasy, Dr. Dave waits until his little girl yields to his every whim before relieving his guilty pleasure.

XXIII

They meet in a coffee shop one block away from Roger's apartment. Li arrives late, knowing he will be there. Upon entering she sees her father's egg-shaped body standing with his back to the door perusing the titles of the well-worn books made available to the patrons of Coffee and Me. She goes to him, and although her plan was to call him Dad, Dr. Dave is what she utters. He turns and sees the girl he adopted so very long ago, and he melts. Her jet-black hair, cut and moussed to a spiky mess frames her gentle features with a hard-edged beauty. She smiles up at him and they hug. He rests his double chin atop her head, and the stiff hair ends of his adopted daughter send a rush of excitement from his chin to another part of his anatomy. They both order green tea and sit on a sofa at the rear of the coffee house.

After a few pleasantries and excuses as to why she did not attend his recent wedding, she asks about Trudy. Li, distracted by her true mission, barely hears the update on Dave's ex-wife, nodding her head as she feigns interest. Dr. Dave seems genuinely happy for Trudy and her brother, saying that for a very long time neither he nor Trudy were happy with one another. Callously, he admits that her adoption was an attempt to deepen their marriage bond, yet it caused quite the opposite effect. Li pays close attention now and figures this is her moment. Waiting for him to take a pause, she blurts out that she is so very sorry.

Dr. Dave, for a brief moment, actually believes a scene he conjured in his mind now plays out before him. Her expression drips with sincerity when she responds to his question of, "What brought this about?"

"I need to rid my life of negativity. Much of it has to do with my feeling that I don't belong anywhere. For as far back as I can remember I've always had this sense that I just don't fit in. I blamed you and Trudy, but now—well, now I realize that you both tried so hard to make me belong but I rejected you both. I'm sorry."

Dave listens and although his mind drifts to those very secret thoughts, he pulls himself back and hears his adopted girl feeling her pain. Things do not go as his lustful thoughts project, and his guilt propels him to agree to aid Li in her quest for closure to her anxiety and pain. They part and as they do, she hugs him while thanking him. Dave's mind rushes to his fantasy place, and patting her atop her spiky blue-black hair, he says, "I'll do what I can. Let's keep this to ourselves, Jerri. Promise?"

"Promise." With renewed hope, the girl known as Jerri Lee to Dr. Dave Lawrence and Li to the rest of the world knows it will all happen. She has seen the look of longing on Dave's expression and just knows he will do just as she wishes.

XXIV

Roger is in a rage. His need to keep this girl blinds him to any rational thought he once possessed. Once his life was simple; he had a wife who loved him and made a lovely home for him and his child. And on the side, an assortment of women who loved the sex they shared. None of those girls held any more fascination for him beyond the immediate gratification of their trysts. He was a teacher in every sense of the word, and once, it seems a very long time ago, he became the student to a girl who devastates him with her announcement that it is over. Repeatedly he pleads with this heartless little wretch who has the downright temerity to offer him Dr. Dave's bloated book on sexual obsession.

She is frightened by his anger and wants him to just go away. It is not so simple. Roger tries everything in his bag of manipulative tricks to hold onto Li. The apartment is hers, he says, as long as they are together. She explains that as soon as she can she will pack up her belongings and move away. He attempts a power play and tells his young Asian beauty she'll have to leave now and to please pack up...he'll wait. Immediately and with no emotion she pulls down two duffel bags and begins to empty her closets. Roger breaks down behind her, and holding onto her waist he sobs against her petite derriere, pleading for her not to go.

She will stay, she says, and Roger weeps. Li does not hide her disgust at his weakness and plays upon it, knowing that once she does pack up and move out she will not return. She waits for Dave to do what he promised, and when her plan bears fruit, she will let the good doctor do what she has seen in his eyes throughout her teenage years. It is curious to Li that these men in her life, these obsessed beasts, are blind to her indifference and are seemingly aroused by her detached demeanor.

The last time she and Roger make love, love is nowhere to be found. He paws at her flesh like a playful puppy seeking out her approval, using all his sexual tricks until he has nothing left. Her boredom with him and this act has her rethinking her commitment to Dave. She knows what to expect from Roger, but with Dave r, Li slightly fears the unknown and does not want another middle-aged Asian fetishist obsessed with her. The act itself is the least disturbing aspect for Li. What she finds most disquieting is their need to possess her, to know all there is to know about her and to keep her like some tame exotic pet.

79

XXV

Within eight weeks, Dr. Dave secures passports, visas and accommodations for two to China. Finding Li's birth mother was not as difficult as the good doctor made it seem. She is still alive, although the same cannot be said of Li's birth father. Xin lives in the tiny village where Li was born and is unaware that Dr. Dave and her only daughter are on their way to China. Although the agency was reluctant to help, Dave finds that money plus celebrity can achieve almost anything. Li hugs him after he tells her what she has wanted to hear all her life: She is to return to China and be reunited with her mother. Dr. Dave just breathes in her embrace; he smells the clean of her hair, the freshness of her youth and is aroused, yet it remains unnoticed by the object of his desire.

XXVI

Xin Peng is swollen. Tears pushed back years ago resurface only to burn. But seeing her only daughter did bring her joy, and those tears did not burn but washed her face anew. Li looks very much like Xin's own mother, and now as she watches her daughter sleep, Xin weeps biting tears at what her selfish wish has done to her only girl.

Li? A last name used as a first, bothers Xin. Li's spirit bothers Xin. It is cold and distant, but it is also hot with anger. Xin cannot help feeling responsible for the girl's demeanor. Xin feels shame. She'd like to lay it at the feet of that oaf of a man who brought her daughter home. But she does not: Xin knows where the shame belongs. This reunion is bittersweet. Xin burns incense at her small altar where a carved ivory Buddha and photos of dead relatives stare at her while she prays for forgiveness.

Ancestors stare through the pungent smoke, admonishing Xin to atone for her selfish act. She remembers Li's birthday with clarity and regret. Xin remembers the pain. She remembers the anger and she replays it in her mind's eye. She prays for forgiveness. She prays to be released from her shame and prays that this troubled soul, her only daughter, will someday know peace.

Xin was glad the doctor refused her insincere offer to stay with them. She did not want him here during her brief time with Li. She sensed his disappointment when her daughter sent him on his way. Xin did not know what they said before the taxi took him away, but what she did know was the way that ox looked at his adopted child, and she did not like what she saw in his eyes. Xin sees discomfort in her daughter's expression as she turns from this father and looks back at her mother. Shame cannot be hidden.

Her daughter stirs and Xin quietly backs away into her kitchen. She sits on the low stool worrying how her son will take the news of his sister's return. Will he see her as an outsider? Li's Mandarin is awkward and Po's Cantonese is fast and local. Will he even attempt communication, or will he dismiss this foreigner with the coldness of his father? Xin has much on her mind. And as she looks about her tiny, immaculate kitchen she once again calls out to the universe, "Thank you for a wish fulfilled. Thank you for my daughter's return. Please forgive me."

THE APPOINTMENT

*Some day, Utterson, after I am dead, you may perhaps come
to learn the right and wrong of this. I cannot tell you.*
— R.L. Stevenson, *Dr. Jekyll and Mr. Hyde*

"Let me in! If you don't, I'm going to the corner, calling for a police officer, and showing him my credentials, and I'll have him and his mates bust down this door."

"No. Go away, Gavin. You can't help. No one can. It's too late."

"You're being ridiculous, Benjamin. Now let me in." Dr. Gavin Montrose raps the carved head of his walking stick on the door with terrific force; small dents appear upon the painted wooden door. He looks up to the sky in frustration, ignores the curious looks from people passing, jiggles at the knob, and punches a gloved fist on the door to 127 East 77th Street. "You're making a bloody spectacle; now let me in."

"If you leave, Gavin, the spectacle will depart with you."

Dr. Montrose knows what to do. As soon as he is inside and has the opportunity, he'll sedate his friend and ring for an ambulance. In this state Benjamin Radcliffe is capable of anything. Gavin, for the life of him, can't understand what's become of his friend. This sniveling, fearful, terrorized, and terrorizing (for there were threats) unfortunate creature behind the door is not the robust and hearty man he's known since coming to New York.

Dr. Montrose can feel his blood pressure rise with each rap-a-tap-tap at Benjamin Radcliffe's chamber door. He goes down the stone steps to follow

83

through with his threat. He turns, and looking up, sees his friend peering through the curtains at the window closest to the door. It's just a moment, and then the figure backs into the shadow, but the visage has Gavin charging back up the steps and once again the tap-taps begin. His voice begins low and stern, "Ben, let me in, followed by, *"Now!"*

Dr. Montrose leans his shoulder against the door, holds the knob waiting for the sound of the lock; he wants to be quick to act before Ben has the chance to change his mind. But there is nothing. How did his friend get this way? Instead of meeting him at the club last night for a late supper and a healthy game of snooker, Ben just may have found his way into Chinatown to partake of some opium. For some it is a fashionable dalliance, smoked every great once in a while…. And for others (for most, really), it is an addictive hallucinogen making the sane plunge into its very opposite. Quite like the insanity that is playing out on these steps, this very morning. Dr. Montrose attempts to turn the knob, fails, and resumes rapping without rhythm, only with steady urgency. Then, in between the rap-tap-taps is a metallic click; the doctor is behind the door, and all is silent.

It is cool in the foyer. Ben crouches near the library doors chewing on his thumbnail. His thick, wavy hair, usually slick with pomade and brushed straight back, is standing this way and that, looking as if Ben has been pulling at it all night long. His whole countenance bespeaks of mental imbalance. His once bright, eager eyes seem vacant as he looks not up toward Gavin but past him—through him. His skin has an unhealthy pallor; jaundice perhaps, or just a need of some sunshine and air. But Gavin was with Ben only last night at the opera, and Ben, as usual, was the picture of perfect health. "Ben." He approaches his friend with caution and a calm voice, so as not to agitate Ben in any way. People suffering withdrawals have been known to be violent. "Ben, come—let me help you."

"There is no helping me, not now—not ever."

"You don't know that. Let the doctor, doctor, and you—well—you do what you do best." He tries to make a joke, "…Beguile the ladies." No knowing chuckle comes back now; only a deep, guttural sound of despair as Ben begins to pound his fist upon the marble floor.

"The ladies…. The ladies." Ben does not mock the doctor with his monotone.

The doctor thinks that in this moment, Ben has seen past him and is now lost inside of his own mind. He kneels on one knee and with his hand soothes his troubled friend by rubbing on his shoulder in an effort to get him off the floor and into the library, where Dr. Montrose could examine him. He knows this man, and secret drug addict Benjamin Radcliffe is most certainly not! Who hasn't tried that blasted Chinese curse? In some circles it's all the fashion. *Dastardly stuff!* He thinks as he prods his friend to stand and ushers him into the library.

The library is darkened by heavy violet velvet curtains drawn over the three floor-to-ceiling double-hung windows. He sits his friend on a tufted chaise that matches the curtains in both texture and tone. The denseness of the curtains is to protect the volumes, some of which are now strewn about the floor, from sunlight and the heat of day. Gavin slowly lets light into this room from the window where just a few moments ago, his once virile friend stood quivering from dementia. "Let me have a look at you." He doesn't dare open the other two curtains, as Ben quakes from just one being drawn. Benjamin Radcliffe shivers in the stream of sunshine that pushes its way across the carpet to brighten the dreary room. A fresh burst of perspiration pours from his skin. With his bag in hand, Dr. Gavin Montrose goes to his friend's side, a bit leery of a man he respects and a man who up until today, was fiercely alive and up for any challenge.

Ben is a large man, both physically and mentally. Large ideas and large dreams were what led Ben to earn his fortune. He is a fearless man with a generous nature. When others quit an enterprise, complaining all the while that it couldn't be done, Ben without worry or argument, went about proving them all wrong. His wealth grows by the day from his foresight and sound investments. But what good is wealth when ill-health robs you of all the pleasure it affords? Ben lets Gavin peer into his pupils, lets him take his pulse, and even lets him check his reflexes. All of these respond dully, with the exception of the pulse, which seems to race a bit, and then slow, only to race again.

Finally, hoping to get a litany of symptoms, Dr. Montrose asks, "So, Ben, what is going on with you?" But the doctor is surprised when his friend grabs his wrist, brings the doctor's hand toward his throat (wrapped tightly in a white silk scarf), and waits as if Gavin will immediately have a diagnosis.

"This. This is what is wrong."

"I don't understand? You'll have to remove the wrapping. Is there an abrasion? Is there swelling? I certainly don't feel any." Without a word, Ben squeezes the doctor's hand at his own neck and with his other hand, pulls the doctor's free hand at and onto his swollen and throbbing member. Immediately repulsed by this action, Gavin tries to extricate himself from Ben's firm grip, and as Gavin looks into his friend's expression, sees his very own reflection in Ben's eyes and is truly frightened. Ben shudders, as Gavin struggles to free himself. Then, Gavin sees in his friend's expression a mania that surpasses anything he has seen before. "Let me go!" Blind ecstasy, pure carnal compulsion, and the more the doctor struggles, the more intense Ben's grip becomes, practically crushing the carpals under Gavin's skin. The intense pressure is steady at Ben's throat and grows firmer with each passing second. Contracting as both hands, his own under Ben's clutch is forced to decrease and increase like a steady throb; a mock heartbeat. Gavin's hand is forced to pulse around the thick shaft covered only by Ben's long white nightshirt much in the same way.

The sound is both of this Earth and quite foreign to the doctor. Gavin has never had this experience before, the witnessing of another man as he completes an orgasm. There are pants and grunts; long vibratory sounds made by air and the straining of muscles. Although he is uncomfortable from this whole experience, his fascination is great. What in God's good earth is happening? Ben lurches forward and shudders violently and then slumps as if his large frame held no skeletal system to support him. His pallor, somewhat improved, begins to return to its sickly gray hue, and as the pressure on his hands loosens, Gavin immediately frees himself and is greatly disturbed. He has a tremendous need to wash his hands, yet they are dry. He looks toward the crotch of his friend and sees that, that too remains dry: There was no ejaculate! There should be evidence through Ben's thin cotton nightshirt, but it is without a stain. Gavin goes to the water closet off the library to wash his hands, although there is no need to do so.

He leaves the narrow door slightly ajar, turns on only the hot tap, and scrubs as if he were preparing for surgery. Unlike his friend, Gavin's complexion is ruddy and falsely robust. Had he not witnessed at first hand this bizarre experience, Dr. Montrose would not have believed it possible. He stares at himself in the mirror above the sink, and beneath his terror lies something deeper, something he may never mention to anyone. Whatever is happening to Ben is serious gravely serious.

Ben seems dead when he returns. He lies on his back, his thick, hairy legs spread wide, and he reeks of musky sweat and something else—something disturbingly, sickeningly sweet.

"Ben…" He shakes his friend's wide shoulders and lightly slap-slaps his unshaven face, "Ben!" His voice is urgent; fearful. Ben's black eyes pop open, exposing whites that are more pink than white. "Ben, what in God's good earth is going on here?"

Confusion sweeps across Ben's face. "God's good earth," he repeats, "God's good earth…. Nothing from God's good, earth…nothing."

"Ben." Gavin tries to lift his friend but cannot; the man is just too big him. In stature the men could not be any more different. Ben is a mountain of a man, broad and solid. Gavin is of an average height with an average build, solid in his own way, but next to Ben, boyish and underdeveloped.

Ben rises and goes to the water closet, relieves himself with the intensity of a racehorse, and lets out a pitiful sound, as if voiding causes him discomfort. Venereal disease affects the mind, the doctor thinks, and his friend, famous for bedding many a great and not-so-great lady, could possibly be diseased. When Ben returns, Gavin asks pointed questions, trying to ascertain exactly what is wrong with Benjamin Radcliffe.

"No. No. No." All questions are answered in the negative. Weakly, Ben walks over to the large wooden globe that sits between two curtained windows, lifts the finial to expose a bar within, and removes a delicate decanter. Alongside it, out of its case, is Ben's Colt six-shooter, and the doctor is concerned, deeply concerned, for both their safety. Without asking, Ben pours the auburn fluid into two glasses. His hands shake as he passes one to Gavin, lifts his own, and consumes it as if it were a glass of cool water. From behind, with the limp robe about his frame, he pours another and downs it as if there is no burn, no alcoholic sting. He turns toward his friend and smiles a curious smile. "If God has anything to do with this then, he is a terrible god; an entity of pure evil, not the forgiving, beneficent being

87

that pastors preach about. What's happening to me is *not* of this Earth and cannot be something of the God they speak about!" Ben has another drink, but he is still sober.

"What…is happening, Ben?"

"I don't know." Ben prefers to doubt his own memory.

He drinks a third drink, looks at the cut crystal in his hand, and shatters the glass by hurling it at a trophy bird long dead but preserved in its natural setting—a tree branch that juts out from a built-in recess above bookshelves that line the west wall. There are no books on that shelf. Beneath this black monster of a bird is a bust of a warrior, slightly gray in appearance, probably from the bluish veins within the marble. Oddly, Ben wears a similar pallor—pale, pale gray.

Gavin rushes to his friend, "Ben! Get a hold of yourself, man! I have a sedative in my bag, but now I'm thinking I'm the one who could use it." Ben drops to his knees and cries; he sobs as if grieving a dead brother.

"Ben, come. Let's get you clean. A hot bath may calm you, and we might be able to figure out what is wrong." Soon they are in the master suite. With the exception of the large painting of a floral arrangement above the marble fireplace, the room is wonderfully masculine. Deep purple walls with a matte finish enclose the room's plutonian serenity. The massive sleigh bed and simple lined furniture is broad and thick, much like Ben himself. Above the door is a carved lintel with a black bird at its center point. The bird is small and has two tiny red glass eyes, only visible when the light hits them just the right way. Gavin has never been upstairs before and suddenly has a pang of guilt, wondering why it took him so long to deduce what could possibly be wrong with his friend.

This thought is brief, but he has heard of some men, men who lead secret double lives, going mad; this could be the case but, Benjamin Radcliff, a latent homosexual? Never! The bath is enormous; all black and white tile in varying diamond patterns. In the center is a stone tub carved from a single piece of black granite with fixtures of brushed nickel Gavin runs only the hot water, allowing steam to fill the room. His friend, still in his robe and nightshirt, stands in the tub, oblivious to the scalding water cascading from the faucet. "Ben." Gavin releases the cold water and hears pipes rattle and bang as the flow grows more intense from pressure. He removes his jacket, rolls up his sleeves, and breaks free of the tight collar and tie around his neck. As if attending a man catatonic, he slips his friend out of his robe, and although he is uncomfortable performing the office, lifts the bottom of Ben's nightshirt in an attempt to remove it. "You're going to have to help me here a bit," he says. Ben turns, bows his head, and lets Gavin remove his garment. At first Gavin does not notice it, but then, much to his horror, he sees something that all his medical training, years of experience, and sane mind are not ready for.

"What's this?" He stares directly at his naked friend with an equal look of both fascination and revulsion. The sight makes him weak in his knees, and he fears he just may lose those few sips of single-malt. There in the tub, clad only in a white scarf tight about his neck, stands his pitiful friend. Even in this state, he is an excellent specimen of man; a Goliath. Handsome, fit, rugged, with a wide muscular chest, dark with hair that only accentuates his masculine form. Statues of gods, long dead and nearly forgotten, have this form; it is the ideal shape of a man. One that Gavin would be envious of if the circumstances were just a bit different. Say, an unintentional glimpse of Ben at the club, where comparisons, either spoken or secret, are always in attendance.

"She did this to me." Ben drops his hand toward his genitals.

"Who?"

"Lenore." His voice fades as if spending the air to express the name wastes him.

"And this?"

Ben begins to undo the tied thin scarf around his neck. And with purely medical purposes, Gavin asks if he may touch this horror that afflicts his friend.

"Wait…Let me remove this. I don't want to repeat the madness from the library." Ben is slow and avoids any contact directly upon his neck. He winces at each unfurl, and now, as Gavin looks away from his friend's genitalia and up toward his neck, he sees a perfect bead of dried blood, reddish-brown from oxygen, staining the scarf. His hand is immediate to examine the thin line around Ben's neck. As if made from the slightest incision, a reddened scar, and perfect in its roundness, traverses Ben's neck.

Ben grasps the doctor's wrist. *"Don't touch it!"*

"Christ, Ben, I'm a doctor." But for all his years of doctoring, this is something completely alien to him.

Gavin turns off the cold tap, lets the hot run a bit more, goes to his jacket and removes from the pocket a pair of buff gloves. He slips them on. "Ben, let me examine it." He leans over the tub and with one hand under Ben's scrotum and the other near his shaft, the physician in him examines what appears to be a second skin encasing Ben's manhood. It is thin like a sheath and has a leather appearance. The color is an iridescent shade of bright, pale green. Mostly to himself he repeats, "What's this? What's this? What's—" He lifts the penis itself, hoping it does not excite his friend. Under it, in pairing rows, are tiny bumps, hard and of a shade of green darker than the sheath. They flank the thick vein that leads to the end of Ben's shaft. He pinches lightly at a pair and can feel them connect with one another like magnets. He looks up at his friend with frightened wonder. "Lenore? Who is she? How did she…?" Again the doctor in him has him do something quick and without reflection. With his left hand he reaches toward his friend's neck and touches the scar around Ben's neck.

"No!" It is unstoppable. Ben reacts with automatic swiftness. Fascinating disgust consumes Gavin as he is once again caught in this frenzy of primal, blind lust. The sound of Ben's climax bounces off the tile walls with the ferocity of a wild animal breaking free of its pen. It is over, and Ben plops himself into the steaming water beneath him.

Gavin is frozen, caught in a bewildering state of confusions not easy to describe. By all scientific logic, he should be covered in ejaculate, but much to his relief, he is not. The thing in his hand had grown to the correct proportion for his friend. But the wild undulations—like tiny worms rushing to the penis head and then back around down the shaft—those were not natural at all. And the swelling at the head had inflated and deflated to an alarming degree. And then there was the color; that odd green shade shifted and darkened from Ben's natural skin tone, giving his member a purple appearance under a thin layer of green.

"Who the hell is Lenore?"

Gavin removes his gloves and ignores them as they drop to the floor. Perfunctorily, he goes to the sink and washes his hands; it seems the right protocol, yet unnecessary, given the gloves and lack of any body fluids. He sits upon the thick lip of the tub looking down and into the water at his friend. Ben's grotesque penis seems buoyant and alive under the ripples.

"Ben! Answer me. Who is Lenore? What the hell is going on with you?" Gavin sees, by his friend's expression, that he gathers thoughts that perplex rather than explain.

"Last I saw you, was between acts at the opera, correct? It was when we arranged our appointment at the club." Gavin nods in agreement. "The wom—" Ben stops himself, shakes his head as if something vile crosses his sight, "The thing—for surely she is no woman—Lenore slipped her way into my box during the finale of *Don Giovanni*. At first I thought she was Sara Thornton. They share a similar figure, especially in that light with only the barest of profiles exposed. I ignored her and watched the massive chorus deliver the poignant end for the sinner. So caught in the moment was I, that when the lights came on I touched her shoulder and called her by name then, realizing my mistake; don't think I wasn't shocked that it wasn't Sara. I was, but the shock wore off quickly when I saw Lenore in her full form. She excused her intrusion by telling me that she, in a rush to witness the end, had entered the wrong box upon returning from the ladies' salon."

"Lenore fascinated me. Her long neck and amber eyes were intoxicating. Much to my surprise, she accepted my invitation to a late supper at Les Vagabonds. I had no idea she would so readily accept, and so I disregarded our appointment. Sorry, old man, but you know—ladies first." Here was a hint of Ben's usual wit, but it quickly disappeared in anguish. "Christ! If only I had kept that appointment."

"She did not whisper a hint of protest when Anton showed us to my usual private dining room. She waited for drinks, which she barely sipped, and, a platter of cold shellfish, which she consumed with the ferocity of, say—" Ben pauses, looks to his friend of many years, "—myself. I drank another glass of champagne and began to devour her. She was more than willing to let me. There were no protestations and false cries of 'please don't' as I fondled and caressed this bewitching creature. Soon, "Wait," she tells me, and asks if we could go to a place where we could go wild for one another. You know me, Gavin. You know of my dalliances. I make no pretense about it."

The doctor did, and if given the same set of circumstances, would have been just as entranced as Ben. It is not often that women of their class were so willing to share their lovely treasures before marriage. Even after the wedding, many of his patients, all men, frequently complained of frigid, fainting matrons who reared their children and used their more womanly wiles as ways to get things from husbands, leaving husbands no other choice than to seek physical gratification elsewhere.

"I brought her here. We were in the library when it happened. It was so freakishly fast and confusing. So utterly fantastic that I thought I was living in a dream—a nightmare, that starts with passionate kisses on her long neck. But within minutes I'm blinded by some thick saliva that, at first, I think is coming from me, and I'm actually embarrassed. I wipe at it and immediately my face is covered with this oozy clear fluid that burns a bit but allows me to have a somewhat blurry vision of what transpires next." Ben slides his head under the water and pops up after but a few seconds. Water streams down his ruggedly handsome face. "It's like looking through water; everything wavers in front of me. Before I can even register what is happening, I'm lifted by the neck and hurled upon the carpet. I am naked and so is she, but now she appears to be in a great green cape and her head puffs out...puffs out...Right in front of me... that beautiful face...puffs out and shifts in front of me. Then I see many images of myself where her face once was! Gavin, I'm mad...I'm going mad! She was not a woman. I try to scream and cannot. I try to extricate myself but am being held down by unseen hands. Both my legs are spread wide apart and my crotch is on fire with urgent lust. All I can remember is the pleasure. The pleasure of being stimulated to the point of animal experience; there is no thought, only instinct; the blind instinct to copulate again and again. That's when I awoke and did think it was all a dream. Then, of course, I looked at myself. Saw this thing at my neck and screamed in holy terror."

The tale is too fantastical to believe. Gavin shudders, knowing that whatever he could possibly assume was wrong with Ben is nothing compared with the reality before him. "And that ring around your neck—"

Ben stops him, "You see what happens when it is touched. She's coming back...I just know it, and I'm scared, Gavin. I'm truly scared."

This is not an imagined terror, like the bug-eyed gaze Gavin has seen in the eyes of the patients in the disturbed ward at Bellevue. This is real. Gavin stares at the sheath with the bizarre bumps. Ben stands unashamed in his tub, and the thing on his crotch seems alive, an entity all its own that has a faint deliberate pulse. The doctor unplugs the drain, releasing the water as Ben pulls on the long chain above, sending a rain stream down his large frame. Gavin gets from a rack two long, thick bath towels and hands them to his troubled friend. Immediately Ben covers his waist and with his other towel dries his torso. Seeing a fresh robe on a door hook, Gavin retrieves it for Ben, pitying him and noting an irony that Ben is all too quick to put into words.

"Odd isn't it? A man with my libidinous past should meet an end like this."

Gavin bravely masks his own fear, "End? Nonsense, Ben. We'll figure this out. After all, it is 1896, I'm sure someone has come across this—" But Gavin trails off, completely at a loss.

Ben screams, "Across what, Gavin? A shape-shifting beauty who imprisons penises, or is it penii, doctor? I did my research. All those books on the floor in the library were not there as a result of passion! The closest thing I could find in all that curious occult material was something called a shape-shifter. Supernatural bullshit created to spread fear." Ben sees something in Gavin's eyes and stops. He dresses in the simplest manner possible. His collarless shirt hangs low past the gruesome thing at his crotch. "I'm sorry, old man. I need a drink." He slips on a baggy pair of trousers that button at the fly and waist.

"Before, Ben, when you voided—when you urinated, was there any discomfort?

"No the bloody thing lets me piss. It feels the pressure and opens as soon as the urine begins to flow. I screamed before because looking at it frightens me! It doesn't come off; it's on there for a purpose." His eyes are moist with fear as he speaks with a distant tone.

"The other thing, you know...my jism does not release, as you can attest to, and it must seem gruesome and insidious to you...maybe I need to apologize for before...I am sorry, friend...but it is the most all-encompassing orgasm; it's like I'm blind with purpose. It is indescribable; like explosions bursting throughout every cell of my being. I am ashamed to admit this: After I awoke and tried to piece things together—the events, I mean—I reached for my neck and was lost for hours masturbating. One hand at my neck, the other gripping my—" He points at the thing below his waist. "Each dry uneventful orgasm was exhausting, yet I am insatiable once the neck is fondled…in any way! Wrapping it up was painful to do; the pressure reminds it that it wants to be fondled, wants to be touched. I say 'it' because this is separate from me…. This is not me!"

Ben is almost screaming as he hurries down the stairs, through the entranceway, and back into the library. He grabs another crystal glass and pours from his opened decanter, offering his friend a drink with a sad nod and somewhat sadder smile. "You have to kill it, Gavin. I'm powerless to do it. She's coming back. I know she is, just know it! You have to—" He drinks, pours, and drinks again. "I thought of just killing myself, but that would be the coward's way out. She'd only go out and do this again to some other unsuspecting lout like me. But why me, I wonder? My size, I think, perhaps, or, would someone like you do, I wonder? You do realize she's using me to—breed!"

Gavin watches his friend and listens to his conjecture, but all the while, his thoughts are stuck on the phrase, "You have to kill it." What if there is some shape-shifting monster, from these quaint books long forgotten? Yet none of these books speak of giant insects with a taste for human sexuality. This is something straight out of fantasy and not real…. But it is real. He believes his friend, for what else could it be?

"Kill it. How? And with what?"

They devise a plan and a back-up plan. If they are unsuccessful, both Benjamin and Gavin will be dead. The blasted thing won't let Gavin live if he fails to kill it. Both men work on the plan long after the sun goes down, eating cold turkey, cranberry compote and bread leftover from the maid's last day of work—was it only two days ago? She is due in tomorrow; she and Dudley will be here, and they may have more of a mess than they ever signed up for. Or, if Gavin is successful, Addie and Dudley will either arrive to, or hear of, the great fire at 127 East 77th Street, New York City.

It is brutal waiting. Both men are anxious in the drawn-curtained, heavily fortified library. They speak in whispers as the night passes. "Never have

I had a friend quite like you, Gavin. Your wit and wisdom over these years remains dear in my heart. Thank you for your friendship. Thank you for this." Ben looks toward Gavin with deep respect, and they embrace like brothers departing at a train depot who know they will never see each other again.

"Ben, if we're quick enough we both can escape this." Gavin looks up at his friend just as they hear a slight tap, tap, tapping at the shuttered windows outside the library. Gavin crouches low and crawls into the unlit water closet. He knows what to do, but will he do it? *I'm not used to such things,* he thinks, and he laughs internally at the stupidity of his thought. Who could be used to something so bizarre? Even if he did slay this supposed creature (for Dr. Montrose still hopes that there is some logical explanation for this...madness), would he be used to it if it happened every day? He doubts it. Now there is a scratch scratching at the front door, and Gavin holds his breath, unaware that he does so. Fear consumes him. Perspiration from his forehead stings as it drips into his eyes, and he wipes at it hearing only the thump-thumps of his own heart pounding in his ears. In here Gavin hears only noise. The code word; wait for the word, and then pounce. But what if there is no word? He hears furniture overturn, hears his friend scream out in terror, but there is no word!

With one hand on the knob and the other on the long pole that Ben himself carved during their vigil to an amazingly sharp point, Gavin Montrose bursts through the door. Nothing has prepared him for this reality. There is his friend splayed out on the carpet. His clothes are in tatters; Ben is mostly naked with that thing on top of him. Ben is caught in some orgasmic nightmare. He pumps, lifting his hairy buttocks and that thing, with its wide head, up and off the floor. The slap-slap-slapping of Ben's buttocks beats faster and faster. The creature bounces from Ben's rhythmic force. Her long rear legs with their thin clamp-shape grip Ben's bare ankles. Her pincer front arms squeeze Ben's thick neck. Ben's nightmare becomes Gavin's reality in a flash. There is no thought, only action, and Gavin is swift. Like St. George slaying the dragon, Gavin, from a crouch, leaps forward, ramming the sharpened pole through the bug's long neck. Her scream is that of a steam engine as it brakes at the station, but the pitch is higher and the duration longer. Her long back leg releases his dead friend's ankle and kicks back, sending Gavin across the room and onto the tufted chaise off to the side of the globe doubling as a bar. And that is perfect. From here it is easy to remove the pistol from the globe and just start shooting. Damn the neighbors!

The thing works at the pole with her front pincers, but all she manages to do is snip off the ends, leaving the pole still lodged in her throat. Gavin hugs the walled bookshelves and makes his way toward her front. He wants to see the thing's face. He wants to be the last thing she sees before he does to her what she did to his friend. Gavin wants to remove the creature's head. He can see himself (him selves?) in the multi-reflective surface of her eyes.... All the Gavins there have the expression of a madman holding a quivering pistol while locked in his own psychosis.

Maybe he only needed a single bullet; maybe all six were necessary. He will never know. The thing's head was all over the library carpet, the chaise, even there on the globe with the hidden bar. Not known for weeping, Dr. Gavin Montrose grieves for his once robust friend. Benjamin Radcliffe's massive body is lying dead under the creature—something that no longer has the countenance of a bewitching female, but instead resembles the shattered remains of a bug.

As if killing the creature isn't enough for one evening, Gavin is galvanized into new action as what at first seems like foam gushes from underneath the horrible creature and over his friend. Each foam bubble swells and shifts as if alive. As Gavin focuses he sees what exactly is inside of each expanding bubble. Is it a trick of his eye or is that a human fetus? Is it an insect? Once again human... and then an insect... *Oh Christ—it's both!* He thinks.

Ben's bodiless head; eyes wide with dead fear stares at this godless scene and it is godless, Gavin thinks. Even if there is such a being, which Gavin highly doubts now, what kind of god would create that...that thing?

If decapitated heads could speak, what would they say? Gavin knows what this one is saying, "Damn it, man, what are you waiting for? You spent a pistol on a tony street in Manhattan. People are coming. You need to flee." Gavin is going mad, for he starts to take directions from the head of his dead friend. "Go back to the water closet and get the kerosene. Do it, my friend. Do it for me. Do it for you and every other man that may have crossed this...thing's path." The flames lick and spread and are quick to engulf the mess on the carpet. Odd pops and high-pitched screeches emerge while Benjamin Radcliffe looks with eyes alive again; alive from the flickering flame. Alive again from the conquest of yet another woman—but this time, his victory was more than for himself.

Will there be questions? People on the street did see him rap-a-tap-tapping at Ben's townhouse door earlier. Will they remember him? That is possible. He leaves through the kitchen and needs to climb over a stone wall to get back on the avenue. He reeks a bit of kerosene, and he likes the smell. It reminds him of something he will never forget: A friendship deep and forged with purpose. He, Dr. Gavin Montrose, just may have saved humankind. No one will ever know, and he will speak of this... nevermore!

BETTE AND MERYL

There's no other person I'd rather be with, no other person I'd rather be loved by, no other person I'd rather love or miss than you!
                                                    —Olivia Williams Diallo

Bette and Meryl share a one-bedroom apartment near the park off West 68th Street. It is a bright apartment with windows on both the north and south sides. The apartment is a steal because of its rent-controlled status, lovingly bequeathed to Meryl upon Nanny Schuster's death. Meryl was caring for Nanny those last few years, so it was only fitting that the apartment be passed on to the devoted granddaughter. Besides, no one else in the family wants to stay in town anymore.

Bette looks down on the people in the street below with two thoughts festering in her brain—two nagging, persistent, awful thoughts that will not go away. She watches the heads of strangers rushing off there to here and back again. She sees three large men in a double-parked truck unload a great deal of unrecognizable things wrapped in bubble-wrap. How she loves bubble-wrap! Bette could pop those bubbles all day. She remembers the very first time she touched the stuff. How different the sound and the texture were then. Now, she thinks, it is pleasantly smooth, like Meryl's skin. Meryl's skin does not react to a little pressure the same way as bubble wrap does, and neither does Meryl. In fact, Meryl usually gives Bette a loving slap, telling her she's "…a bad girl!" But Meryl doesn't mean it. Bette knows the bond between them is deep, impenetrable. Distractions are fleeting things!

Bette wonders if Meryl will ever return, and her anxiety grows by the minute. She knows all too well how dangerous those streets are. Just last week, a yellow cab plowed into a group of pedestrians, right outside their window. She thinks of these terrible things and shudders with each different scenario as they play out before her. *Where is she?* Then that other thought, the one Bette hides deep, deep inside: Maybe Meryl left her; left her alone to die here in this apartment. *Maybe she found someone she likes better and will never return. Please, let it not be a man.* How Bette hates men! They've never been nice to her for as long as she can remember.

She lets out an exhausted yawn, feels the sunlight warm on her body, and lies there waiting. *Please,* Bette thinks, *let me hear her key in the lock. Let me hear her familiar step. Please send Meryl back to me.* And with these thoughts, thoughts of a loving reunion, Bette rests her eyes and sleeps. Not that heavy, deep sleep—no, it's that other sleep; that sleep in which the mind drifts from memory to fantasy with endless possible predictions. There is no real rest from that sleep.

It is the radio that arouses her from her slumber. Maybe she did go to sleep, as there is a slight dampness at the corner of her lip from drool. She brushes it away, yawning to give herself some energy. *Where is Meryl? Where did she go? Why couldn't she take me?* Then she thinks better of that idea, knowing how travel and she just did not get along. Far too much stress for Bette! The ride to the sea, that different house with all those bugs, and, oddly, a noise most enjoy, is irksome for Bette. The pounding of the sea is something she loathes. *Give me the city, even if it is only from this window! If I want the country, I'll look down upon the courtyard and its lovely garden.*

In spring it is alive with activity; plantings and cook-outs with select neighbors taking turns. It is all so civil and community oriented. Meryl likes going down there; Bette not so much. Outside makes her too anxious. She has made it known, in the most certain of terms, that she will have no part of it. During summer, birds nest in a tree outside the dining room window. It amuses her to watch the bright blue eggs hatch. And to see those initially ugly, but progressively beautiful beings develop to eventually fly away. She would love to hold one, if only for a minute, if only to feel its little heartbeat race and then watch it fly away. Meryl says she can't have one. Bette resents her for that and other things as well. In fall the leaves turn and the garden is alive with neighbors helping to enrich the soil for next year. They have a building party where food is served, all homegrown, and it pleases them. For Bette it is fun to watch, but she does not enjoy the garden's bounty.

Bette thinks she likes winter best of all; especially from that window. In winter, it is easy to see into other apartments, and that always fascinates Bette. Wondering how they live, who they are—all of it keeps her ever-ready mind active with assumption and speculation. Also, with no leaves upon the trees, those birds come to feed from feeders diligently maintained by Mr. Norman Sparks. Norman is about the only man Bette tolerates. Norman has never shown a nasty side, like his friend Arthur.... Bette hates Arthur for no other reason than his countenance. Arthur looks like a man from long ago who tried to hurt her. There's something she hates thinking about; that awful man with the hairy face, coming toward her with his hot breath wheezing at her pushing her into the other room. That's another thing she resents Meryl for; Meryl let it happen.

Bette likes to think it is she who broke Meryl and that jerk up and hopes in her heart that Meryl is through with men. *Where is she though?* Then a most terrible thought flies in between her ears: *What if Meryl is still seeing that jerk someplace else? Could it be? Could that be the reason she is not here? She is off somewhere snuggling with that hairy-faced creep.* This infuriates Bette, and as she ruminates over each scenario of betrayal, her breaths become rapid. She lets out a tiny cry as if her torment is reality: Meryl will leave her never to come back.

It is not healthy to be in her head with these thoughts, and they do not abate. Bette's resentment grows silly and petty. Why does Meryl only call her by her given name when she arrives home? "Babette," she'll call after the door opens. It's always the same cadence; always the same tone, "Baaa-Bette, where are you?" As if she is hiding? As if today is the day Babette somehow left the comfort of 57-B in The Westwick Apartments on West 68th Street? Never!

———

Meryl Keith waves good-bye to her colleague, knowing she is late. Babette will be furious. There will be the cold dismissive attitude that shows its ugliness whenever Meryl has been gone this long. She can't believe that after caring for Nanny Schuster, she now worries about Bette in much the same way. Nanny was a lot of work with her demands, and so is Bette. But it is different. Meryl stops at the gourmet shop, picks up a roasted chicken, premade salad with ginger dressing...*That ought to be enough,* she thinks. Then she stops at the cheese section for some herb-crusted Brie, knowing that both the chicken and a little bit of cheese just may appease the petulant Babette.

Maybe it is age, but Bette is all too comfortable with her routine, and, like Nanny, needs a reality check every once in a while. With her groceries in her all-natural hemp bag, Meryl stops at a little bistro on the corner of Columbus and 69th to sip a gimlet before she heads home. Le Chat Noir was all the rage when Nanny first moved to that apartment. Now it is a comfortable place serving authentic country French cuisine. Besides, it was the very last place Nanny wanted to go before she became too sick to go out any longer. The icy lime smoothness pleasantly chills her with the warmth that only alcohol provides. Her drink is good. So good, in fact, that she orders a second and, while waiting, is approached by her longtime male companion, Jack Creighton.

Their brief affair, long over now, is a painful reminder of just how lousy Meryl is at relationships. Their friendship is solid and will probably last a lifetime, she thinks. They go to business functions together as each other's dates and usually have fun. Now, at this chance meeting, they hug and exchange pleasantries. She tries to buy Jack a Guinness, but he is too quick to pay.

"Can't you ever just accept that it is I who am the gentleman, and a gentleman never lets a lady pay?" he says, smiling. Meryl leans close to him and whispers something in his ear that makes his ears grow red, and his face contorts into a rich laugh. "No, I guess you ain't...no lady.... Not with that wicked tongue!" They laugh, drink, and do a bit of catching-up, "I met her online. We've been seeing each other almost every day. She has her claws in me, and I like it."

"Jack, I'm so happy for you." And she is most sincerely happy. "A November engagement,—how lovely. Does she know you're going to ask her?"

"She may suspect something. My, but it is good to see you! You look well."

"Don't feel well. I don't mean to complain, but work isn't as much fun these days. The whole place is in a tailspin. The new director...what a jerk..." Meryl hears herself drone on about the recent shift at her job. She hears herself describe her disillusionment with a place that fifteen years ago was progressive and exciting to go to every day. She hears herself denigrate her new boss, much to Jack's amusement. Jack knows of the new director by reputation only and listens, chuckling at every snide remark.

Meryl feels the alcohol cool her anger. She drifts back to her apartment and to Bette. The day has been long, and here, with Jack, Meryl thinks that if she accepts his offer of another drink, she just may throw herself at this engaged man from her past. Jack was always good for an "attack in the sack." She fondly remembers their brief affair. Remembers how well versed he is in the art of pleasing a woman, and that is dangerous. Meryl remembers Nanny's staunch view on casual sex: "She is a hussy! And he—well, dear, most men are dogs. They sniff around a lady's drawers until the day they die, unless," she'd always chuckle, "unless you burn their smeller!" It has been too long since Meryl has been with a man, and as her mind drifts, she hears herself refuse the third gimlet, all the while longing to just go home to Babette.

They part at the bar with promises to see each other "real soon," and laugh at the pretense. The evening is misty with rain that floats instead of hurling itself to the ground. The mist holds the scents of the city, and Meryl wonders about the beach house. Will her brother Tommy be closing it this year? If so, maybe she'll join him. Bette will be a stress but it will be worth it if only to be far away from the office for a day or, perhaps...five! Lost in thought, she crosses the street, heading home strictly on autopilot.

Oddly, the vile exhaust from sluggish traffic entices her to have a cigarette. It's been years, but the desire won't ever leave, especially when she indulges in a drink or two. It is tempting, but she knows a single one may lead her back to a pack a day, and that is simply out of the question! Babette wouldn't allow it. She laughs at this thought, remembering all the shredded packages and loose tobacco strewn about the apartment. No, she cannot stop at the newsstand to buy them. However, she can stop and buy some

Necco Wafers, perhaps an Almond Joy for later, when she and Babette are snug on the couch with the flickering glare of the television as their only source of light. It is Thursday.... She likes a program and can't remember if the damn thing is on tonight. Or did she miss it? She'll have to check the listing.

Nanny, on Thursdays, liked to watch the news magazine shows. Babette doesn't much care as long as they nestle, side by side. Meryl begins to plan her night: First, feed Babette, and then herself. After, soak in a hot tub with Babette by her side. Pity Bette can't scrub her back, but such is life. *It's funny,* Meryl thinks. After Nanny died she felt desperately alone. She had thought relief would sweep over her now that her responsibility to Nanny was through, but going back to the apartment was depressing. Babette changed all that. Meryl knows that caring for Bette is far less demanding than caring for her Nanny, although Bette does need tending. That fills her life with purpose. Yes, going home to an apartment housing many memories is more pleasant now that she is with Babette.

From this distance, and with the mist covering the city, Babette thinks she sees Meryl at the newsstand. Her heart leaps with recognition, and knowing Meryl will be home any minute, Bette feels it race with excitement. She yawns and starts to think that maybe, just maybe, she'll ignore Meryl to punish her for being so late. After all, without Meryl, Bette would not be able to feed herself; that is the cause for most of her anxiety. Her resentment grows as she watches Meryl walk toward the Westwick Apartments. She shudders at the memory of the sound of her given name that Meryl uses only when the door is open and Meryl is finally home. *Maybe I'll hide,* she thinks, and shakes that silly thought away deciding instead to feign sleep. That'll teach Meryl. No greeting at all—just a weakened arousal and perhaps a disinterested approach to whatever is for dinner. *That's what I'll do,* she thinks.

Meryl looks up toward her apartment window and sees the shadow of Babette; then she is gone. Not really thinking, Meryl steps out, not at the corner, but midway through their block. The sound of screeching brakes and the impact makes her lose her step, and down upon the pavement she goes.

———

Babette hears the tires screech and rushes as best she can back to the window. *Oh no!* She thinks, letting out a howl as if something sharp stabs at her heart again and again. She sees that yellow cab. She sees the driver get out in a panic and sees Meryl still holding her briefcase, splayed out upon the ground. Stuck here in the apartment, Babette is helpless and her worry increases as people crowd around her beloved friend and companion. She shakes her head, hoping that when she looks down upon this scene again, it somehow will be different. Bette hopes that is not Meryl. Please, she thinks, let Meryl be locked in the arms of that man with the hairy face! Bette prefers that awful reality instead of the horror from the window.

———

Meryl does not know what hit her. As her eyes burst open, her memory and cognition come back in a flash. A man in a turban is speaking in half English and half—well, his native tongue. A well-dressed woman is telling her not to get up. She should lie there and wait for an ambulance. She feels the bag beneath her, knowing the chicken is probably staining her hemp bag and possibly her suit. She internally checks herself and knows that other than some bruising she will be fine.

———

Oh! Please get up, Meryl. Please! Babette lets go of all her resentment, but her anxiety increases with each passing second. Then, a miracle: Meryl gets up on her knees and, with the help of the man in the turban, is standing wiping at her head. She shakes her arms a bit, takes her crushed packages and attaché, and makes her way through the crowd.

Now comes the familiar sound of key in lock and now Babette hears the, "Baaa-Bette! Where is my only girl?" *Should I rush to her? Or, should I just lie here and pretend I didn't see the accident on the street?* A faintly familiar odor wafts into the apartment, and it is that scent that changes Babette's mind in a flash, and not the fear of just moments before when she thought Meryl to be hurt, or possibly dead.

She stands arching her back, letting out a river of meows that say more than, "Welcome home." More than, "So glad you're not hurt or, dead, for that matter!" And so much more than, "Where the hell is my chicken?" No, while Babette purrs and weaves through the damp legs of her companion and friend Meryl, each purr, every rub, and all those meows say: *"Heureux, heureux à en mourir:* Happy, so happy I could die. *Je t'adore, mon amie:* I love you, my friend."

Made in the USA
Charleston, SC
31 August 2014